Early Praise for **THE LONGSHOT**

"In the sparest, simplest prose, *The Longshot* takes the reader into the minds, hearts, and bodies of two highly dedicated and taciturn men. Kitamura's descriptions of mixed-martial-arts fighting are brutal yet beautiful. She builds tension, uncertainty, and even fear. . . . Her story is compelling, and her writing is spellbinding, both in its power and beauty. This is one of those novels that catches the reader by surprise. Kitamura is a genuine discovery. Expect to hear much more from her."
—*Booklist,* starred review

"Hemingway's returned to life—and this time, he's a woman."
—Tom McCarthy, author of *Remainder*

"Back in the day, we'd have wondered how a woman—a woman!—could know so much about this brutally masculine world. The marvel today is that Katie Kitamura can write about it with such grace, compassion, and breezy confidence. She knows her way around the ring and the human heart."
—Elizabeth Benedict, author of *The Practice of Deceit*

"Katie Kitamura has written a novel as terse, elegant, thoughtful and economical as Roy Jones, Jr., on his best days. Her writing is spare and graceful, her ear for dialogue precise, and she writes with the kind of controlled, compressed passion that produces literary gems."
—Jon Fasman, author of *The Geographer's Library*

THE LONGSHOT

A NOVEL

KATIE KITAMURA

FREE PRESS

New York   London   Toronto   Sydney

FREE PRESS

A Division of Simon & Schuster, Inc.
1230 Avenue of the Americas
New York, NY 10020

First Free Press trade paperback edition August 2009

FREE PRESS and colophon are trademarks of Simon & Schuster, Inc.

For information about special discounts for bulk purchases,
please contact Simon & Schuster Special Sales at 1-800-456-6798
or business@simonandschuster.com.

The Simon & Schuster Speakers Bureau can bring authors to your live event. For
more information or to book an event contact the Simon & Schuster Speakers Bureau
at 1-866-248-3049 or visit our website at www.simonspeakers.com.

DESIGNED BY ERICH HOBBING

Manufactured in the United States of America

1   3   5   7   9   10   8   6   4   2

Library of Congress Cataloging-in-Publication Data
Kitamura, Katie M.
The longshot: a novel / Katie Kitamura.
p. cm.
1. Martial arts fiction. 2. Sports stories. I. Title.
PS3611.I877F54 2009
813'.6—dc22
2008040501
ISBN 978-1-4391-0752-2
ISBN 978-1-4391-1760-6 (ebook)

For Taki,
with thanks

THE LONGSHOT

1

He stood just under six feet and he was cleanly proportioned. He'd been cleanly proportioned the day Riley met him and nothing about that had changed in the ten years since. He had soft eyes and an open face and that was the same too. He had changed in the body. His bones had hardened and he walked with the rolling gait of a fighter. Looking at him now, he couldn't be anything but. That was the biggest change.

They drove down to Tijuana three days before the fight. Riley knew a place where they could practice and the motels in Mexico were cheap. He figured they could do with an extra twenty-four hours getting used to the place. They left at ten. Cal fell asleep as soon as they hit the interstate. That was fine with Riley. He had his thermos of coffee, and there was the radio. As far as he was concerned, the more sleep Cal got the better.

He remembered they used to drive clear across the country, chasing down fights. He'd drive for hours with

Cal sitting beside him like sleeping dynamite. It was a feeling. Driving into a fight with the win already in place. It made the drive easy. He'd drive and he'd watch the feeling spread out all around him. Like he had a million bucks riding with him in the car. That used to be the feeling of it.

That wasn't the feeling now, but he didn't mind. He looked out the window. There was nothing alongside the road except for gas stations and car dealerships and the occasional Best Value Motor Inn. Like all of America was about the driving. The road hardly swerved and the other cars were just coasting along. Riley kept at seventy. He didn't think he changed lanes once.

He drove until his back was sore and the car was running low on gas. He looked over at Cal. The kid was sleeping sound and he hated to wake him by stopping so he kept on driving for another twenty minutes. The landscape outside was flat and dry and scorched by the sun and the feeling, as he drove along in silence, was very gentle. The gas meter hit empty. Riley edged the Jeep over one lane and barreled down an exit ramp.

Cal woke as the car slowed. He sat, blinking slowly and staring out the window. Neither man spoke as Riley swung into a gas station and stopped before an empty pump. He switched the ignition off. The engine sputtered for a moment, then fell silent.

"Gas," Riley said. He looked at Cal. "And you should stretch your legs. Make sure you don't cramp up sleeping like that."

Cal nodded. They both got out of the car.

"Gotta take a leak," Cal said.

Riley nodded. He didn't look up. "Go ahead."

Riley stared at the ground as the tank filled. He listened to the gas glugging through. He listened to the numbers clicking.

"What kind of mileage you get with that thing?" Cal was back.

"Shit."

He clicked to an even thirty dollars. Then he dropped the nozzle into its stand. He screwed the gas cap back on and knocked the door shut.

Riley looked at Cal. He was leaning with one hand against the car. He was still yawning. He nodded to Riley.

"You have a good time in Vegas?"

"You know how it is. There were a couple good fights."

"I heard Vera looked good."

"He looked real good."

"How'd things go with Duane?"

"He got the win. We found a nice little weakness in Diego's game. You could tell from the tapes he dropped his right hand, so I told Duane to go out there and jab. Take him to pieces. It worked."

Cal nodded. He stared at the car, shifting his weight. Riley smiled.

"Come on. Let's get going."

"You need money?"

"Don't worry about it."

"I got money."

"I said, don't worry about it."

Cal got into the car. Riley followed him. They drove out. A couple seconds and they were back on the freeway. Riley flicked on the radio.

"You still listening to this crap?"

"Fuck off."

Cal grinned at Riley, then looked out the window. He sat with his hands resting on his legs and he watched the landscape flash by. Riley glanced out the window. He thought California looked pretty much the same, everywhere along the freeways. He looked at Cal. He was still staring out the window.

"Get some sleep."

Cal didn't respond. Riley looked at him again. "Get some sleep," he said. His voice was gentle. Cal nodded. He looked out the window a bit longer. Then he settled into his seat with his head pillowed against his arm. Pretty soon he was asleep again, breathing slow and regular. Riley sat back, satisfied. He continued driving south.

As they got closer to the border the color drained out. He never saw the color changing but it faded right in front of him. A couple more miles and the landscape emptied out too. The buildings disappeared and the overpasses vanished and it changed the proportions somehow. There was a lot more sky. Riley couldn't even see the road in front of him. All he could see was sky.

The radio crapped out just past San Diego. Then the

signs started turning up. Signs selling car insurance. Signs selling bail bonds. Riley clocked them as he drove. They were like a countdown to the border. He drove past the signs advertising stateside parking and the ones advertising shuttles across the border. He saw a big board, written in capital letters. LAST EXIT USA. After that the road funneled into Mexico and the border hit him in the face.

The dirt jumped out. The people did too. The signs and the lights and everything else. Every time he crossed the border and dropped into Mexico he felt the difference right away. The crossing happened quick. The cars sped through on a six-lane road and they didn't even slow. There was nothing at the border stopping them. Border Patrol just sat in a bunch of black Jeeps and watched as the cars poured into the country.

Riley glanced out the window. There were people everywhere. He could see the vendors cluttering up the street selling ponchos and plastic figurines and bowls of fruit. They were scuttling around and they were hustling for their work. He didn't know what that said about Tijuana. He thought about Mexico and he thought about Tijuana and the two didn't seem the same. It was like staring at the border so long had made Tijuana different.

Cal was up again and looking around. He seemed restless after his sleep. He craned his neck to stare out the window. He fiddled with the lock on the door, tapping it with his fingers.

"So this is Tijuana."

"Yeah. This is Tijuana."

"You know your way around?"

"Sure. I've had a couple guys in fights down here."

"Good thing I got you around."

Riley glanced at him. "That a thank-you?"

Cal smiled. He shrugged. "Sure," he said. "Okay."

Riley shook his head. He concentrated on driving.

They turned down the Paseo de Los Heroes. There were a bunch of crazy monuments and a bunch of crazy roundabouts on the boulevard. Driving was a fucking nightmare. The street was packed with cars. Nobody stayed in their lane and anyway the lanes just disappeared at every roundabout. There was a roundabout every thirty seconds it felt like. Riley tightened his grip on the wheel and he jerked them down and around the road. His shoulders only dropped once they turned off the boulevard and cut down toward Agua Caliente.

One street over and the city looked totally different. The California license plates disappeared. The bars and clubs dropped out into tile shops and auto repair garages. The tourists never made it off Revolution Avenue. They never made it past the margarita bars and the donkey carts. Drive a couple blocks and Tijuana started looking like any other deadbeat town, just with everything written in Spanish and everybody driving a little bit more reckless.

They were staying at some motel a couple streets away from the Caliente, some place called the Playas. The pro-

6

moters used it because it was close by, but Riley figured the place came with a warning. It came with words like "basic" and "convenient" and "local." Polite words telling them they were putting them up in some nameless dump. Well, he knew there wasn't any such thing as a luxury motel in Tijuana, and Riley wasn't the kind to fall for a name, but still—a Motel 6 would be nice. Some place with a 1-800 number you could call when your valuables went missing. He'd bet this Playas joint didn't even have an in-room safe.

He swung into the motel parking lot. He guessed the tourists were turning up everywhere nowadays. He could smell the crew cuts and the surfer shorts before he got out of the car. The paint was peeling and there was a balcony running down one side of the building and he could already imagine the kids congregating on it with their beers. He pictured beer cans floating in the pool out back. He pictured loud music. He pictured spring break—Riley snapped the ignition off. If there was noise late at night he was going to shut it down, and personally. Cal needed to sleep solid.

The place looked deserted when they walked in. There was a bell on the counter, and a sign reading "Please Ring For Service" in English and Spanish. The handwriting on the sign was a little wobbly but it was legible. Riley dropped his bags on the floor and looked at the bell. He slammed his palm onto the bell once, twice. He did it a third time.

After a minute, an overweight man appeared behind

the registration desk. He was breathing heavy and his shirt was soaked in sweat. Riley frowned.

"Can I help you?"

"Yeah, we're staying for a few nights."

"You got a reservation?"

"We got a reservation. We're paying for the first night. The TFL's paying for the rest. They should've sent you a memo or something."

"Sure. Fill this out, will you?" He pushed a registration card across to Riley.

Riley leaned into the counter and began on the card. He wasn't so big anymore, but he was still pretty imposing. He was even more imposing when he wasn't feeling friendly, and the guy wasn't making him feel friendly.

The man remained placid. He looked at Riley. He looked at Cal. Riley straightened up and handed the card to the man.

"So," he said as he examined their registration card, "You boys are here for the fights I take it."

"Yeah, we're here for the fights," Riley said. "You follow fighting?"

"Hard not to when it's happening so close." He shrugged. "Should be a good night. Rivera alone is worth the price of admission. The rest of the card could be total shit and you'd still have a sellout."

Riley pressed a finger onto the registration card. "About that rate. I was given a quote of forty-six dollars. Nineteen dollars off the rack rate."

The man nodded. He examined the registration card. He put it back on the counter and crossed it with a pencil. He resumed talking.

"I wasn't a huge fan of fighting until the first time I saw Rivera fight. Blew my mind. Never seen anything like it. I figure every fight fan can remember their first Rivera fight."

Riley cleared his throat noisily. "Another thing. Can you get us a room that's quiet? As far away from the pool as possible." He nodded at Cal. "The kid needs to sleep."

The man shuffled round slowly and examined the keys hanging on the board behind the desk. He picked out a pair and turned back to face them. He nodded to Cal.

"You fighting Saturday?"

Cal nodded.

"Well, forget what I said about the rest of the card, will you? I haven't really looked at it yet. Not closely."

"That's okay," Cal said. "It doesn't matter."

He smiled at the man. The man beamed back at him.

"You know how it is. It's a pretty big thing, having the champion fight down here."

"Like you said. The guy's a legend."

"The man's the whole sport. Nobody can touch him."

"I guess not too many guys can give him a fight."

Riley glanced at Cal. "Look, we're sort of tired out from the drive. Maybe you could just confirm that rate of forty-six dollars a night, give us the keys and we'll let ourselves in? Like I said, forty-six dollars a night—nineteen dollars off the rack rate."

"*Sí, sí.*" The man nodded. He came out from behind the desk and picked up Cal's bag.

"I'll take it," Cal said.

"No, please." The man shook his head and smiled and then began walking down the hall with the bag. They followed him. "This room is a good deal." The man spoke over his shoulder. "You will see. It is a nice room—with a balcony!"

Riley was frowning the whole walk up to the room. Cal just kept nodding every time the man said something.

The man let them into a room on the far end of the second floor. It wasn't so bad, and it was far away from the pool. Inside, there were two double beds, a couple of dressers and some chairs. The man gave them the key to the minibar and told them there was a decent restaurant next door where they could get breakfast. He told them to give him a call if they had any questions. He clapped Cal on the back and shook his hand. He wished him luck. Then he backed out of the room and disappeared.

"*Sí, sí.* Asshole speaks English better than I do." Riley dropped his bags onto one of the beds. "Why'd you talk to him like that? I couldn't pin him down on the rate with you being all friendly and making conversation." He kicked the door so it closed with a slam and starting unzipping his bags.

Cal looked at Riley's bags. "You didn't tell me you were moving down here."

"Smart-ass."

Cal looked around the room, then sat down on the other bed. Riley began sorting through his bags, pulling out piles of clothes and gear.

"I'm gonna have a shower."

"Okay."

Riley yanked out some shower things and threw them onto the bed. He hummed to himself, some tune from the radio. He paused and looked up at Cal.

"By the way—why didn't you tell him?"

"Tell him what?"

"That you were fighting Rivera."

"Oh," Cal said. "I don't know. I was embarrassed."

"Embarrassed? You?" Riley snorted.

"The guy thought he knew about fighting."

"He didn't know shit about fighting."

"He wanted to shake my hand," Cal said.

Riley waved a shampoo bottle at Cal. "Well, he's gonna feel like a real fucking idiot once he finds out who you are. The guy who took his boy Rivera the distance." He disappeared into the bathroom.

"That was four years ago," Cal called out after him. "Nobody remembers that shit anymore."

Riley slammed the bathroom door shut. Cal sighed. He stretched out on the bed, hands folded behind his head. He kept his eyes open and he listened to the sound of the showerhead. When Riley came out of the bathroom, he was in the same position, staring up at the ceiling.

Riley sat down on the bed. He looked at Cal as he toweled off his hair. "Well, here we are. Fuck of a drive."

"Yeah. You were right about getting it out of the way."

"What do you feel like eating?"

"I don't know."

"We could try the place next door. Might as well."

Cal nodded. Riley placed his hand on the bedside table, palm down. He cleared his throat and looked around the room.

"I guess it's not so bad. The room."

"It's pretty decent."

They were silent. Riley nodded to Cal.

"How you feeling? You looking forward to it?"

"Sure I'm looking forward to it."

"Well, it's just a little longer."

"Yeah." Cal sat up and ran a hand over his face. "Yeah." He stood up. "Okay. I'll shower, and then let's go eat. I'm feeling pretty hungry."

Riley nodded. He sat for a while after Cal went into the bathroom. Then he stood up and walked over to the window. He pushed the curtains back and stared outside. There was nothing to look at except the parking lot and the motel sign. The letters looked watery and they were blinking unevenly.

"Christ. I don't believe it," he said. "Our first night in Mexico and it's raining."

2

The first time he saw Cal it opened up a feeling. A big feeling, like a road running out to the horizon. He just took off down that road. He didn't look back. He didn't even think. He just grabbed the kid and ran. The feeling went off in his head. The rest of him was still watching the kid. The rest of him was standing there, just trying to take in the way he worked.

It was a high school wrestling room pretty much like any other high school wrestling room. Only a couple guys had turned up for practice. The place smelled like feet and sweat and the fluorescent lights buzzed the whole time. The semester had ended. Graduation was a week away and the place was barely running.

He stood. He watched. He kept looking for flaws. He kept thinking he wouldn't be able to keep it up. Being so good. Being so full of the talent. Riley could barely breathe with it. He was afraid he'd blink and miss something. He kept watching and pretty soon it was like he couldn't remember what it had been like before he'd seen him. It was like the kid had wiped out his memory of everything else.

When practice ended he went up and introduced himself. He talked to the kid. He was about to graduate high school. He wasn't going to college. He was thinking about taking a job at the hardware store. He had a rack of wrestling medals in his bedroom, but he figured they weren't going to do him much good in the real world. That's what he said to Riley.

Riley listened. Then he talked. He told the kid to come to the gym. He said there was money to be made. He said there was a life to be made. A life that was more than some hardware store. The kid looked at him. He listened. He said he'd have to keep the job at the hardware store. He said he couldn't give that up. Riley told him he could keep the job. He said he could keep it for now.

Riley thought a year. He thought a year of training and the kid would be ready for his first fight. He was wrong. The kid scored his first knockout the second week of practice. He let out a big overhand right from straight out of nowhere and the other guy was out cold. The whole room went quiet. They stared at the kid. He looked back at them. "I didn't mean it," he said. They kept staring at him. "I don't know what happened," he said.

One month and he was looking as good as guys who'd been training for years. Three months and he'd outgrown the team. Riley had picked the kid for his wrestling skills.

He'd picked the kid because of his ground work. Knock-out power was a bonus. Knockout power like the kid had—that was the kind of bonus you prayed for night and day. That was the kind of thing you waited for a lifetime.

After three months he figured he was ready for a fight. He booked the kid local. He trained him hard. He got the kid ready. He knew this was the test. Some guys couldn't take it out of the gym. The first time was the hardest. You saw things the first time. Before the fight Riley was so nervous he had to make a run for the bathroom. He hung his head in the toilet and hurled up his stomach twice and then he felt better.

The kid knocked the other guy out in twenty-three sec-onds. Riley watched him from the corner. He counted the seconds. He counted them out and by the time he reached twenty-three and the other guy was falling to the canvas his heart was racing and a part of it was sinking too, because he figured this was it. Cal was the one. The kid had everything a fighter needed and if he didn't become champion then Riley would have no one to blame but himself.

Driving home after the fight, Cal said, "So I guess I'm pretty good at this, huh?" Riley shook his head. He said, "That's a good one." "Surprised?" Cal was smiling as he spoke and he looked so pleased with himself that Riley had to shake his head again. "Yeah," he remembered say-ing. "Yeah—you had me pretty surprised back there." After he said it Cal had looked even more pleased. Then he'd become embarrassed. "It's not really a big deal," he said. "I knew I'd be good at it."

Well, the kid was good at it. There was no other way of putting it. He was good at it and pretty soon it was like the game was happening to him instead of the other way round. He kept going up. He went up so fast that Riley started thinking maybe it would never end. He started thinking maybe this was the way it was. Maybe that was when everything changed. He started getting used to it— and then the way it was just died on them.

It was still raining in the morning. After they ate, they walked through the rain to an empty warehouse down the road. The street was quiet and the dust was tamped down by the wetness in the air. The buildings stood half a foot crooked and the sidewalk crumbled into the street. They had to concentrate to walk and then they got used to it. The door, when they arrived, was chained and pad-locked shut. Cal waited as Riley reached inside his pocket and brought out a set of keys. He picked one out and fit it into the padlock. The door was stiff and the hinges creaked when he shoved it open.

Inside, the air was cool and fresh. The room was bare apart from a few bags and a wrestling mat laid out on the concrete floor. Riley looked around the room. He tossed the keys into the air a couple times. Then he shoved them back into his pocket. Cal dropped his bag onto one of the aluminum benches resting by the door. He turned slowly, stretching out his back and arms. Then he sat down on the bench and pulled his bag open. Crossing his arms, Riley watched as Cal slid his sandals off and began taping up his feet.

"Doesn't look like this place's been used for years."

"It's okay."

"Bet Rivera's got digs a damn sight different to this."

Cal didn't look up. "He'd better. With the purses he's bringing home."

Riley sat down beside him. "I heard they're giving him upward of eight, nine hundred thousand to fight. You hear that too?" He shook his head. "Man, you could open a gym for every fight. Have a whole chain of 'em, all across the country."

Cal stood up and stripped off his sweatshirt. He looked at Riley. "We gonna get started or what?"

Riley nodded and stood up. Outside, the rain continued falling.

They warmed up. After stretching, they began with a basic warmup. It was an old routine and their movements were paced as they sent a single jab, a hook, sailing through the air. The jab doubled into twin jabs, then into three-punch combinations, then into three-punch combinations ending with a knee. Their movements grew crisper as they began adding in turns and half-turns, sudden lunges to the ground and rapid leaps back to their feet.

Before too long a thin film of sweat was coating Cal's body and he was breathing lightly from the mouth.

Riley nodded, satisfied. "You look good," he said.

Cal looked up, pleased.

"How long you run this morning?"

"Half an hour."

Riley nodded. "Come on. Let's work the mitts a bit."

Riley held the mitts for Cal, moving in an irregular circuit. He swooped from left to right, jaw-high down to the liver. Cal hit the mitts square. Each blow echoed brokenly through the warehouse and then was muffled by the next. The sound was good. It was even and clean. Riley grunted to himself. He began moving faster, pushing the blows down, springing the mitts back up. Soon they were working at tremendous speed. Midway through, Riley switched to pads and they began working the legs. Cal landed his kicks square and hard and he kept his balance loose and easy.

Riley motioned to Cal to stop and tossed the pads aside. Cal walked over and picked up a pair of shinguards. He strapped them on and then he straightened up and adjusted his gloves. He picked at the ties, drawing them close.

"How are the girls?" Riley asked.

"Yeah, they're doing good."

"You get to see them much?"

Cal shrugged, head down. "I got them every other weekend."

Riley cleared his throat. "Okay, let's go."

They sparred lightly for one five-minute round. They paused. Riley nodded. "Come on," he grunted to Cal.

They began again. Cal moved sharper, faster, working combinations, weaving cautiously, locating the lapses in Riley's concentration. He moved quickly, more like a welter than a light-heavy. He jabbed twice, clean through the guard. He landed a right, a left, and then threw a knee straight to the body.

Riley ate a lot of the shots. Immediately his movements improved. He gave Cal a hard shot to the body. Before he could follow it up, Cal was blocking and giving counterblow to blow. He worked the body again, two hard shots to the liver. The overhand right that ended the combination sent Riley staggering back a few feet.

"You okay?" Cal called. He said the words like he was standing far away.

Riley nodded. "Yeah," he said, bringing his hands back up.

Cal nodded to himself. He bounced lightly on his feet, hands down. He moved into the setup for a kick. Riley sprang forward. Cal batted his glove away and walloped him with another stinging overhand right to the jaw. Even with the gloves, Riley felt the blow go shivering down his spine and to his feet. Riley had been in the ring with some pretty good fighters. The kid hit harder than all of them. With four-ounce gloves and in the middle of a fight, a punch like that could knock a man out of the game.

"You fell for that one," Cal said, smiling.

"I didn't fall for nothing," Riley muttered.

Cal laughed quietly to himself. "I got you with that one."

"Always a joker, huh?" Riley said. "Always got something up your sleeve."

They continued, hitting full force. They had to. There was no other way to prepare for a fight. There was no other way to get the reflexes sharp enough. If he had the choice, Riley would have had a young fighter take his place. Someone green. Someone who still had something to learn from being knocked near senseless. The shots were making his head gummy and he had to force himself to concentrate. He shivered and dodged another one of Cal's looping overhand rights.

When they stopped, Cal was moving lightly on his feet. He looked contented as he bounced in place, then came to a stop. Riley was breathing heavy. He leaned against the wall with one hand.

"Right." He straightened up. "I'm getting too old for this."

Cal was watching Riley. He smiled.

Riley glared at him. "Go and hit the bag for a minute or something."

Cal nodded and retreated to the bags.

Riley watched him. He carried most of his weight in the back and shoulders. The muscles along his neck and arms and shoulders were built out and now, as he slammed his fists into the bag, they sprang together in bunches.

"You put on a bit a weight for this?" Riley called out sharply.

"A couple pounds. Five, maybe. Did a bit of lifting."

Riley frowned. "Lifting?"

Cal paused and steadied the bag. "I don't know. Felt a bit weak or something."

"Don't get me started on lifting—"

"I know," Cal said.

Riley nodded to himself. "Come on. Let's see how your ground game's coming."

They moved to the floor. Cal fell to his back with a sigh as they began rolling. Even with his wrestling background, the kid was always happier on his feet. Riley had been known for his grappling and he had taught most of what he knew to Cal. In the end that had been everything except the willingness to go for a submission victory. Cal always wanted to knock them out. Even in practice, it was like he couldn't wait to get back to his feet. Rolling with Riley, he had developed a pretty perfect defense against submissions. Riley knew it was the most he could ask for.

"What you grinning at?" Riley breathed.

"Nothing."

They continued. Riley slipped on a pretty good armbar. Cal grinned, gap-toothed.

"What you grinning at?" he repeated. Riley's voice was irritated.

"Nothing. You got nothing."

"What about now?" he said. He shifted position, exerting a bit more pressure on the arm.

"Still nothing."

"Now?"

"Nothing."

They were breathing heavier. Rotating, Cal got himself out of the armbar. Riley guessed the escape would impress the judges nearly as much as the attempt itself. He grunted appreciatively. They fell back to the floor, breathing heavily.

"Back there, I gave it to you," he said to Cal after a moment.

"I know."

"I gave it to you but you fell back."

"I know."

"Why?"

"Dunno," he said.

Riley was silent for a minute. Then he stood up. "We should go again," he said. Cal nodded and straightened up, still breathing deep.

Later, they sat slumped against the wall.

"How's Clem?" Cal asked.

Riley shook his head. "Yeah, he's not doing so good."

Cal nodded. "That's tough."

"You know how it changes people," Riley said.

Cal nodded. People always said that a bad knockout changed a fighter. They said before it was like sailing.

They said after you could see how the game worked. After you could always just tell in the ring. Cal had never been knocked out but he figured he knew what that was like. He guessed he knew the feeling.

The guy could have made a good fighter. Cal had watched him a couple times at the gym. He was strong and his technique was solid. He had good instincts too. Still young. They had pushed him too quickly.

Cal stood up and walked over to the benches. He sat down and slid his feet into his sandals.

"He fighting soon?" he asked, head down.

"Nah. He says he doesn't want to rush things this time."

"You should get him back in the ring as fast as you can."

"Yeah, I know. But he doesn't want to. You can't make a guy fight when his heart's not in it."

"How bad was it?"

"Pretty bad. He didn't know what hit him." Riley stood up and followed him across the mat. Idly, he kicked at the leg of the bench. "Kid didn't even know what it felt like, losing. It was a bad way to find out."

"He's tough. He'll be okay."

"Nah." Riley shook his head. "He was tough so long as he was winning. Kid's scared now. He's talking big, about how next time they meet he's gonna whoop Craig's ass for him good, how he's gonna show him it was just a lucky punch, but it's all talk."

"Craig's at the top of his division."

"We thought he had a chance."

They walked out. Cal watched as Riley slipped the chain round the handles of the door. The rain had stopped.

They began walking back to the motel. Riley turned to Cal. "I thought maybe after the fight, you could come in and do a couple of clinics."

"Okay." Cal shrugged. "Sure."

"Maybe talk to Clem. Spend a bit of time with him. You know how he looks up to you."

"You sure there's any point?"

"What do you mean?" Riley asked. He looked at Cal, irritated. "Sure there's a point. There's always a point."

"I thought you said he didn't want to fight."

"I said—what I *said* was, he doesn't know if he wants to fight or not. Kid doesn't know right from left anymore, that's how bad he got mashed up. What I'm asking is for you to come in and help him make up his mind."

Cal shook his head. "Okay. Yeah, of course I'll come down."

Riley was silent for a moment. Then he clapped Cal on the back. "Anyway, we should be concentrating on you, right?" He grinned at Cal. "We should be concentrating on your fight."

Cal nodded. He shrugged out his shoulders, restlessly.

"You're looking good, kid," Riley said. "Best I've seen you in a long time." He paused. Cal didn't respond, other than to nod again.

They reached the motel. The man from the day before

was asleep in his hatch, an old baseball cap drawn down over his eyes. Their key hung in an empty row on the board above. Riley reached across the sleeping man and palmed their key. He gave the guy a look of disgust as he moved away.

"You see that?" Riley asked as they walked up the stairs to their room. "Anybody could just reach over and grab our keys. Break in and steal all our stuff."

"Not got anything to steal."

Riley glared at him. "I'm serious."

"I know. You've been taking things too serious lately."

"Yeah, well, you just look your things over real careful. Make sure nothing's missing."

The room was untouched since morning. The two double beds lay unfurled, and yesterday's clothes hung over the backs of chairs. There was a stale smell inside. Cal crossed the room to open a window.

"You see?" Riley bellowed. "What time is it? Twelve? Twelve noon and the maid's not even cleaned the room." His voice was loud enough to hear down the hall.

Cal ignored him. "I'm having a shower." Riley nodded to him absently. He was still muttering to himself.

When Cal emerged from the shower, Riley was on the floor, plugging in a video player. He looked up at Cal. "Got the tapes."

"You brought a video player?"

Riley paused to look up at him. "Sure I brought a video player."

Cal rubbed a towel across his face. "Which ones you got?"

"The last five."

"Seen those already."

Riley didn't look up as he slid a tape into the player. He stood up.

"There's no point," Cal said.

"Sit down. It's playing."

The television blinked restlessly and then jumped into focus. Rivera stood on the ropes, head crowned in sweat, fists high in the air in his trademark sign of victory. Cal watched him thoughtfully. Most fighters raised their fists after a good win; he did it himself. Rivera actually punched the air, so that the air around him seemed to gain density as his fists whipped through. The crowd roared and streamers fell from the ceiling and the belt was strapped back around his waist.

Riley frowned and peered at the controls.

"Was just watching them the other night—got to rewind a bit."

"It kinda takes the suspense away, doesn't it?" Cal said. "Knowing he's gonna win."

Riley ignored him. Cal sat on the edge of the unmade bed and looked at the screen.

"Who's he fighting?"

"Sanchez."

He stopped the tape and pressed play. Rivera strode into the center of the ring for the touching of the gloves.

He had a short, choppy stride. His body vibrated with motion. Rivera never conserved his energy. He never fought with three rounds in mind. In the early days it had been part of the psychology of his style. It was only later that the way he burned his energy seemed like the manner of a certified champion. Cal could almost see it. He could almost see that he was fighting with a big purse and an early night in mind.

He watched Rivera walk up for the staredown. All he could see were his eyes. They blocked everything else out. A murmur ran through the stadium. The fight hadn't even started and the crowd was giddy just watching.

"Without a doubt, Rivera's got the best staredown in the business," said the fight commentator. "Let me tell you. Rivera wins his fights at the staredown."

"Fucking bullshit," Riley muttered. "I can't believe they pay people to come up with this fucking bullshit."

Cal shrugged. A lot of people liked to say that Rivera won his fights at the staredown. Rivera made things easy to understand. There was nothing simple about a fight. But watching Rivera, pretty much everything about the game seemed obvious.

The tape played. Rivera bulldozed Sanchez from a distance of six inches. Sanchez looked spooked, though he had to have known coming in about Rivera's staredown. Sanchez shifted his eyes to one side and then the other. He looked up and down and finally he just looked at the ref.

Riley shook his head. "Still. The man's got a point. You know right there that poor fucker's gonna lose."

"The staredown means nothing. It's a waste of energy." Cal watched the screen. "Rivera's the only good fighter who uses it." Riley shrugged.

The fighters retreated to their corners. The bell rang. They sprang forward and then halted, each just beyond the other's carefully assessed reach. They circled. After all Rivera was not without respect for Sanchez's game. The ref called for action. Rivera threw a low right kick that nearly knocked Sanchez off balance. It had a mean snap as it connected and Riley sucked in his breath, wincing.

Rivera lunged forward on the follow-up. Wary, Sanchez retreated.

"You see that? You see how he's dictating the pace of the fight?" Riley snorted. "How's the kid gonna fight when he's running away? You can't fight when you're walking backward. He's not even letting him get into his game."

Cal nodded. Rivera landed a right straight to the body. Sanchez threw a clumsy counterpunch that left him walking into another right straight. They backed away from the exchange and circled. Rivera landed the right kick again. Sanchez was nursing a bruise on his left leg and a mouse under his left eye. Both would serve as good targets for Rivera, and Rivera was not the kind of fighter who needed targets to aim. It was only two minutes thirty into the first round and already Sanchez looked like he had run through his game plan. Rivera looked like he had just started his. Cal could see Sanchez thinking on his feet. It was never a good sign.

Sanchez shot in for the takedown. Rivera's sprawl was flawless—that was another thing he was known for. Sanchez flung his arms up to protect his head. Rivera landed a few good knees to the head before Sanchez got him off. Somehow, Sanchez managed to connect with Rivera's head as they straightened to their feet. Cal leaned forward.

"Sanchez hit hard?"

"Rivera can take a punch."

"Nah, he gets dinged pretty easy."

"You're talking about *your* punches. With *your* punches, most people get knocked out. Rivera, on the other hand—he just gets a bit dinged." He paused and then repeated, "Rivera can take a punch."

"That's cause he recovers fast," Cal said thoughtfully. "He recovers real fast. He gets rocked, but he's back in the game before you can do anything with it."

On screen, Sanchez struck Rivera, through the guard and square on the chin. It looked to be the hardest strike Rivera would receive in the fight. He immediately closed the distance and locked Sanchez into a clinch.

"See? Look at that. He had him there for a second. He should have followed it up, worked some knees."

Rivera slammed Sanchez to the ground in a takedown that made the ropes tremble. Sanchez looked like he had spent the bulk of his energy in that earlier takedown attempt. He'd gassed on nerves. From the guard, Rivera softened him up with some body shots before moving to full mount.

"Oh no," Riley groaned. "You don't want to *give* Rivera full mount like that."

It was only a few seconds before the ref stepped in to end the fight. Riley grunted and leaned forward to eject the tape. Cal looked down at his hands, then blinked.

"What's next?"

"Sierra."

"Not worth watching."

"They're always worth watching." Riley paused as the tape began. Rivera was giving a prefight interview for the camera. Some girl was doing the interview. She was pretty, but she was doing a good job of seeming competent. It looked like maybe Rivera was flirting with her, Cal couldn't tell.

Riley snorted. "Man. He's one ugly bastard."

"At least he doesn't have to worry about losing his looks."

"Like the rest of us?"

Cal laughed.

Riley shook his head. "Crazy thing is, I figure the guy's getting uglier and uglier as the years go by. First time I saw Rivera, I thought, Man, they don't come any uglier. Was I wrong. It's getting so his face is all blurred up from the punches."

"Must be in practice. He's not getting too many kisses in the ring."

The video jumped to the fight. They watched as Sierra entered the ring. He circled round, bowing to the audience and mugging for the cameras. The audience cheered him on. He was what they called a crowd favorite: he earned his money before the fight began. At least he looked like he was enjoying himself. You could almost see the shadow fall across his face when Rivera made his entrance.

Just walking down the aisle, Rivera looked mean. He had his hood up and something about the light made his skin look chalky white. His eyes were squinting and his jaw was cutting hard against the blue light and he looked in no hurry to get to the ring. In his corner, Sierra was pacing restlessly. One of his cornermen clapped him on the shoulder. He nodded back, blinking.

"Well, it's a good knee. I'll give him that."

"Fucker shouldn't have rushed him. Never, never rush a fighter like Rivera."

Rivera stepped into the ring. His hood was down and the lights were up and he looked in bad temper. He was glaring all around him—at his own corner, at the ref, at the judges sitting ringside. Somebody in the crowd screamed his name and he glared up in the direction of the call.

"Somebody's not playing."

Cal nodded. Sierra met Rivera at the staredown with a

bug-eyed stare of his own. The crowd roared approval. Rivera shook his head in disgust as they retreated to their respective corners. He was still shaking it when the bell rang. Sierra burst out of his corner and came rushing toward Rivera. Rivera stood and waited and then he took a step forward and kneed him in the head. *Whack!!* It was a direct hit and Sierra lay sprawled out on the canvas. Rivera walked away. He didn't even check to see if Sierra was out. The ref chased after him to raise his hand for the victory.

"Eight seconds."

"That's like, what—a hundred thousand bucks a second?"

"Yeah. Once you see the highlight you've seen the whole fight."

Riley popped the tape out and put in a new one. The next two fights were more of the same. Neither put Rivera in trouble. Neither made it past the first round.

Cal sat back as Riley sorted through the tapes. Across the fights the competition was varied. Sierra was a joke, but Sanchez wasn't half bad. He figured Johnson and Silva were both top contenders at the time of their fights. It didn't matter. Rivera left the playing field leveled behind him. He always had. Any fighter stepping into the ring with Rivera was going to be outclassed. Any fighter stepping into the ring with Rivera was going to lose.

There was a monotony that set in whenever they watched his fights like this. Every single fight was alike.

The losing was in the air, long before the bell rang. Cal could feel it, even on tape.

Riley slid in the last cassette.

"What's this one?"

"Murray."

"Let's see it." Cal cleared his throat and sat up.

"I've not watched this since." Riley sat down. "Don't know what it was, but it's like he had a hard-on for the kid from the start."

"Maybe cause he was with us," Cal said. Riley nodded. The tape clicked and then started playing.

In the first few minutes of the fight Murray gave Rivera more trouble than he'd seen in a long time. He tagged him a couple times, he had him moving backward, and Rivera didn't know what it was like, moving backward. The first few minutes it didn't even look like a Rivera fight, that's how good Murray was doing.

Cal leaned closer toward the monitor. Murray was moving quick, avoiding Rivera's punches, getting the counterpunch, jamming up his rhythms. He could see the confidence in Murray's face as he shut down another one of Rivera's takedown attempts. Rivera started to look frustrated, and that should have been a good sign. The bell rang out and they retreated to their corners.

The first round went solidly to Murray. Sounding embarrassed, the fight commentators put forward the notion of an upset, then immediately dismissed the possibility. In their corners, both fighters looked fresh. Riley was saying something to Murray as he rubbed him down and Murray was nodding back. He looked eager for the second round.

The second round began. They had two brief exchanges to welcome it in. Murray got the better of both of them. He looked ready to go. Then Rivera changed tactics. He started sitting back into himself, waiting for Murray to attack. He feinted and then did nothing. He circled round, looking wily. Just doing nothing he was throwing a wrench into the fight. It went against everything they knew about him. Everything they knew said that Rivera did not fight in the counterattack. Rivera did not wait for holes; he smothered his opponents instead. Cal couldn't remember the last time he had seen Rivera standing quiet in the middle of the ring.

Without Rivera being aggressive it was like there was a huge vacuum in the ring. It was like there wasn't anything to make the fight out of. Murray started to get confused. The ref called for action. Murray attacked, and then attacked again. It was like he couldn't think of anything else to do. That's when Rivera caught him. He started landing the body shots. He started hitting the legs. Murray looked like he didn't know where the strikes were coming from. It wasn't the kind of fight they had prepared him for. Cal remembered sitting in the corner feeling heartsick.

Two minutes into the second round Rivera knocked him out with a vicious one-two combination. Murray crumpled to the ground, mouth slack. Rivera pounced on him. He landed three clean shots to the head. Brain damage shots. The ref dodged in, gesturing for a stop. Rivera pushed him aside as the bell rang. He lifted his foot—a head stomp holding the ropes. Murray's head bounced hard on the mat. One, two, three times. Chaos ensued as the respective corners flooded into the ring. Cal caught a glimpse of Riley, a shot of himself. Refs, judges, doctors, security—in an instant the ring was packed tight. Watching it on screen, he realized how quickly they had all moved. In the end it took eight guys to hold Rivera back. Even when things had calmed down and he had taken the trophy and strapped on his belt, the expression on Rivera's face was one of frustration. He looked fresh, almost like he hadn't fought at all. Down on the mat, Murray wasn't moving.

Riley didn't look at Cal as he snapped the television off. "I'm gonna have a shower," he said. He retreated into the bathroom, leaving Cal alone. Cal stared at the television screen. Then he flopped backward onto the bed. He needed to sleep.

3

Cal slept most of the afternoon. Riley shook him awake around five and they walked back down the road to the warehouse. This time it wasn't raining, and the air was cool with dusk.

They had a light workout scheduled for the evening. Cal jumped rope to warm up. He liked it—he liked the feel of his feet bouncing on the mat and he liked the rope arcing around him. He kept his arms taut and his hands rotating quickly and soon his feet were skimming fast over the mat. The rope made a high whistling noise as it soared through the air and then a light slapping sound as it hit against the mat. Riley watched him for a minute. Then he stepped outside, pulling the door shut behind him.

He could hear the whistling and the slapping as he stood outside the door, breathing in deep. The air was nicer than in the morning and he decided he would walk to enjoy it. The streets were wide and poorly lit and the buildings decrepit but the air was still nice. Down at the far end of the street the bars on Revolution Avenue were starting to spill light and outside the restaurants waiters were setting up wooden tables. He stood and watched them as they spread white paper tablecloths and secured them with metal clamps. They smoothed the paper with their fingers and then they laid out plates, napkins, forks and knives. He heard somebody set down a heavy crate of bottles with a shout; the glass clinked and jostled in a friendly way. Overhead, peeling billboards with broken mouths and missing eyes were printed in Spanish and English. He read them. *"Radio La Preciosa,"* he mouthed out quietly. *"Con Mas Recuerdos."*

He wished they'd skipped Murray's fight. He hadn't been thinking. Cal had been right there in the ring with Murray. He'd believed in Murray, or else he'd believed in the game plan and believed he knew a way to get to Rivera—either way Riley knew there'd been a lot of believing, gone into that fight. And Cal had taken the fight personal. They never discussed it, but he knew he'd taken it personal.

He'd sent Murray in to feel out Rivera. To get a sense of what he was doing in the ring. Watching the tapes was always different to being in the ring. Nobody knew a fighter better than the last guy in the ring with him. Riley figured they could learn a lot from Murray fighting Rivera. But Murray hadn't been able to tell them anything. He couldn't remember the fight. He couldn't answer a single question.

Riley watched Murray falling. He saw him hit the canvas, and some part of him just stayed there in the ring. But he had to move past it. What mattered was getting Cal back on track. People were starting to forget about the kid. The telephone was ringing less and less. The kid had to get back on track, and a rematch with Rivera was the best way of doing that. With or without Murray's help.

Riley believed in the rematch. Cal was the only fighter to go the distance with Rivera. He was the only fighter Rivera hadn't knocked out. Riley believed in the rematch so much he'd held off asking for it. He knew they'd only get one chance. That first fight with Rivera had set Cal back. It had taught him what it felt like to lose. Riley figured he needed time to get his game together. That time had run out. It had run out while he'd been looking the other way, and the stakes had jumped up. Now a rematch was the only thing that would get Cal back on track. It was the only thing that would make him a contender again.

He stood in the corner. He watched Murray falling, and more than ever he was sure it was the right time. The rematch would make people see. It would make them remember how good the kid was. People forgot easy, but Riley figured it didn't take that much to get them remembering. The rematch would get them remembering for sure. Cal would do good against Rivera. Riley knew Cal. He knew Cal better than he knew anybody.

After the fight, Murray had been rushed to the hospital and they ended up spending the next three days staring at

Murray lying in a hospital bed. He was fine. He had some busted-up ribs and a broken hand and a badly dislocated shoulder, but mostly the doctors were just being cautious. Riley stood on one side of the bed and Cal stood on the other and they looked at Murray. Riley tried to think of something to say but it wasn't easy. He looked at Murray and he looked at the bruising on his face and around his collarbone and he thought about Cal. He was thinking about Murray and he was thinking about Cal and he tried to keep it from showing. He tried to think of something to say.

Murray looked at him thinking of things to say. Riley looked back. Then Murray opened his mouth and asked them when the doctors thought he'd be able to get back to training. They had to laugh. There he was, sitting in a hospital bed, high off his head and already he was talking about training. Then they stopped laughing and went back to looking. There wasn't going to be any more training. Murray was finished. It struck Riley. It was ugly but his next thought was he hoped Murray's loss wouldn't affect the scheduling on Cal's rematch. He surely hoped it wouldn't.

Riley shook his head. Murray was starting up a business now, looking after people's yards. He'd got his girlfriend pregnant and he seemed pretty happy about that. He stopped by the gym now and again to say hey. Some days Riley looked at him and he thought maybe after all it had been for the best. It had ended. The kid had got set free from the game. He was happy. That was something. He guessed for sure that was something.

Riley turned and walked back to the warehouse. He put the thoughts out of his head and kept his mind clear. He wasn't gone long and when he returned, he could hear the same light slapping, only now at a faster pace, so that the sound of the slaps blurred into the hum of the rope flying through the air. The sound was high and nervous. Cal nodded to Riley when he entered, maintaining pace. He continued for a few more minutes before coming to an abrupt halt. He was breathing light as he dropped the rope from his hands. It jumped up once, then shivered to a stop on the floor.

They sparred five three-minute rounds, working light. Cal's reflexes were looking good. He'd pulled them to a point and he was moving in full fight mode. He was shuffling fast. He danced and then he worked little flurries and then he danced some more. He shuffled and he kept his chin tucked in neatly and he kept his hands up and his eyes focused and he released flurries of seven, eight punches. Hooks and straights and crosses and uppercuts, all dropped in together. They came to a halt.

"Okay," Riley said. "You're moving good, kid."

Cal smiled. "Thanks."

Riley paused. He pulled off his gloves and tossed them to one side. He looked at Cal.

"We done with the sparring?" Cal asked.

"Tell me about Ohio."

Cal shrugged. "It was okay."

"Walker's got some good guys. You pick up some things?"

"I picked up some things. I worked on my takedowns. They got some good wrestlers."

"Let's see what you got."

They started on their feet. They circled round. Riley surged forward with a right; Cal shot in and scored the takedown. On his back, Riley blinked. The kid was *fast*.

They got back to their feet. Riley was ready for him; this time they clinched up. Cal scored a single-leg take-down. The next time it was a double-leg. Cal flipped Riley up into the air and then blanketed him on the mat. Next he showed him improvised judo throws. Wrestling slams. Single-leg trip takedowns. A few he purely muscled, and that was impressive too. Every time, Cal got him down and he pinned him fast.

They stood up. Riley nodded to Cal.

"Okay. You've been working on your takedowns."

Cal nodded.

"You got fast, kid."

"I was always fast."

"Yeah, okay. You got *good*. How's your sprawl?"

"It's good. Like always."

"Let's see."

This time, Riley worked the takedowns. He shot in, hard and fast. Cal slipped into a perfect sprawl, legs flying back and arms clinching round Riley's chest. He leaned in against him with his weight. He squeezed the air out of his lungs. He hummed a tune as he mimed knees to the head. Riley shook him off.

They worked it maybe close to twenty times. Out of those twenty times, Riley scored exactly two takedowns. Once he got the takedown, Cal kept him tight in his guard. Riley was strong working from inside the guard and even so he couldn't gain position and he couldn't score damage points. Cal's grip was strong and there wasn't any way a thinking judge wouldn't stand them back up within the minute. The other eighteen times, Cal sprawled so perfect it was hard to see how Rivera was going to avoid eating a lot of knees to the head. If things went Cal's way, he'd be able to dictate whether the fight stayed standing or went to the ground. If things went his way.

Riley went thoughtful. Cal didn't say anything. They packed up their things and left, locking the door behind them.

They decided to eat at the restaurant next door to the motel, same as the day before. The place was called Dixie's. The menu was vinyl and filled with surf 'n' turf, steak, chicken burgers, tacos, margaritas, Coke floats. It came with a sheet of photocopied pink paper listing the specials. The specials came by the month.

Inside, the restaurant was empty. The light was fluorescent but it was dim. They were seated at a corner booth.

Riley opened the vinyl menu. He flipped the pages restlessly. Then he folded it back up and set it down, folding his hands on top of the table. Cal looked up.

"I'm going to have the holiday platter," Riley said.

Cal nodded. "Yeah, I thought that looked pretty good too."

"Okay." Riley craned his neck round and motioned to a waitress. She came over and pulled out pad and pencil.

"Two holiday platters." Riley held up two fingers, then pointed to the item on the menu.

The waitress nodded. "Anything to drink?" Her English was pretty fluent. Down here everybody's English was pretty fluent.

Riley looked at her suspiciously. "Just water." She nodded and drifted away.

Riley looked at Cal. "Okay, so you've been working on your takedowns."

"Surprised?"

"Not as surprised as Rivera's gonna be. That double-leg you've got is something. How long you work on that?"

"Pretty long."

"Got bored with everything else?"

Cal nodded.

Riley shook his head. "Okay." He leaned forward across the table. "We gotta discuss your game plan."

"Okay."

"You got anything figured out?"

"Nah." Cal paused. He shrugged. "You know I'm not a

game plan kind of a guy, Riley. Just like going out and seeing which way the fight wants to go."

"A game plan could do you good against Rivera."

Cal nodded.

Riley cleared his throat. "I've been thinking about it, seeing the tapes again and seeing how you've developed your game." His voice was excited. "Think I got something. Something that could work."

"Let's hear it."

"First things first. Rivera hasn't gone the distance since the fight with you, and that was four years ago. I looked at the stats. He's ended ten fights in the first round, four in the second. Most of those early on." He looked at Cal. "Guy doesn't know what it's like going the distance."

Cal frowned. "He doesn't go the distance cause he doesn't have to. He's always had good cardio. I'm the one who gassed. Not him."

"You gassed because you went into that fight with one week's notice. Strictly speaking, you should never have taken that fight. This time's different. This time you're in peak condition. Your cardio's perfect. And anyway, that fight was four years ago. *Four years!* That's a hell of a long time. A lot has changed since then. You watch his most recent fights and you can tell he's getting tired. You can tell he's in a hurry to get the knockout cause he's worried all the time about gassing."

"Go on."

"I always figured the key to winning with Rivera is jamming up his rhythms. You watch him fight, he's following a rhythm. He just flows—left, left, right, knee to the head, knee to the head, shot to the body, shot to the body. When that rhythm gets broken, he starts slugging it out. Gets wild. Now, that's pretty scary too, but at least it opens up holes. At least it gives chances."

Cal nodded. Riley leaned forward. He tapped with a finger hard on the tabletop.

"I want you to open up the round jabbing. Rivera is going to expect you to come out swinging. Looking for the knockout with that crazy overhand right of yours. I want you to do the exact opposite. I want you to box. I want you to pick your shots, I want you to *think*. Use the counterattack to jam his rhythm up. Get him so he's expending energy throwing haymakers, trying to catch you. You don't want to knock him out—you just want to get him irritated. Break his calm."

"We did that with Murray," Cal said. "And we know how that turned out."

Riley ignored him. "Now. Listen up. Even when he's wild, Rivera's dangerous on his feet. We've seen it a thousand times—he's swinging wild and then he catches the other guy and then all of a sudden his game shapes up. All of a sudden he's throwing straight and he's thinking strategic. *You do not want to stand with Rivera.* It's too dangerous. The guy can sneak in a knockout from just about nowhere. As soon as you see a hole, you go for the takedown. You fall on him, and you don't let him get back up."

Riley slapped one hand flat on the table to illustrate the movement. The water glasses slid an inch, then stopped. Cal nodded.

"Once you're on the ground, keep him there. Use your weight to cut his air off. Lean on him. Tire him out. Work the body shots—you want to inflict the kind of damage that's gonna cost him in the third round. And whatever you do, keep him on his back. Neutralize. You score a couple points. More important, you keep *him* from scoring points. Don't take stupid risks. The man's got good sweeps. Do just enough not to get stood back up."

Riley paused for a moment. He looked up at Cal. Cal's eyes were soft and alert. He continued.

"Okay. Second round. He's tired out. He only fought into the second round once in his last six fights. Six fights! That's a year. That's over a year. Now. First of all, I want you to save the right hand. I'm not saying don't use it." Riley spread his hands out, palms facing upward. He shook his head. "I'm not saying don't use it. I wouldn't ask that of you. I'm just saying, don't use it *yet*. Save it. Keep working the jabs. Then, take him back to the ground as quick as you can. Keep him there, and keep softening him up. If he gets up, you bring him back down. Hell, bring him back down whether he gets up or not.

"Of course, Rivera's a smart fighter. He's tough, and he learns quick. After the first time, he's gonna be watching for the takedown. But keep switching up and keep using everything you got and you might outsmart him yet. You don't need to outsmart him forever, just long enough to get into the third round. Now, you push things into the third round and Rivera's gonna be tired. He's gonna be frustrated and he's gonna be confused, cause he doesn't know how to fight somebody else's game. Everything you threw at him in the first two rounds is gonna start showing. That's when you explode. That's when you start working the knees. That's when you start throwing your haymakers. And then you use that big right hand, *boom*. End it right there."

He spread his hands out again. The air vibrated with the victory he described. For a moment, both he and Cal stared at his palms. They had a broad reach. His fingers were long and roughed with calluses. They both stared at his hands without saying anything. Then Riley folded them up and they rested on the table.

A game plan worked like a story that a fighter told to himself again and again until he believed in it, and Riley was a good storyteller. He looked at Cal. He looked at the kid thinking.

Inside his head, Riley reviewed the plan. He'd half been thinking aloud, but he knew it was decent. There were two things that made a game plan solid: the relative ease with which it could be executed, and the relative ease with which it could be remembered. Riley knew the real purpose of a game plan was to set down a steady post and leave it there. Leave it there in case the fighter needed something to cling to come the rush of the fight. It was just dropping down anchors. It was just trying not to drift out too far.

Riley thought about it. He was pretty sure the game plan could work. He had a good gauge of both Rivera's weaknesses and Cal's strengths. Match them against each other and you had a game plan that would work. You couldn't beat Rivera standing. Nobody had ever done it, and plenty had tried. Take it to the ground, though, and things started to look possible. He had good takedown defense, but if you could get through that, and he was pretty sure Cal could, if you could get him down and keep him there—he looked at Cal. He was still sitting there looking thoughtful.

He said, "It's a good game plan."

Riley nodded, but he was tired around the eyes and he did not look directly at Cal.

Their holiday platters arrived. Mexican flags had been taped onto toothpicks and stuck into their steaks. They pulled the toothpicks out and ate the low-grade steak and lobster and potatoes and corn on the cob in silence. There was a basket of bread rolls and Riley sliced them into halves and made steak sandwiches. The grease from the meat flavored the bread and the rolls stayed crusty when he bit into them.

Riley said, "You think this is for Mexican Independence Day or something?" He twirled the toothpick flag between his fingers and tried to smile.

Cal smiled and shrugged and didn't respond. He kept eating. He cleared his plate and then said he would eat something for dessert. Riley cleaned his teeth with the toothpick flag. He shredded the paper flag and drove the toothpick blunt.

He jerked his chin at Cal.

"You talk about a game plan with Walker and those guys?"

Cal looked up. "What?"

"You talk out a game plan, while you were in Ohio?"

"No." Cal looked startled. "Why?"

"I mean, it would have been normal. With the fight coming up and everything. It would have been normal, if you guys had talked about it."

Cal shrugged. "We didn't discuss it."

They ate their desserts and then they stood up and paid the bill. Cal was due for an early night, ten hours' sleep if he could manage it. They walked out of the restaurant. The air outside was warm. Cal stared up at the sky. He frowned, as if he were thinking.

"I think I'll keep it standing," he said to Riley.

Riley nodded. "Sure, kid," he said. "Sure."

"I don't know," Cal said. "It just feels right."

They continued walking back toward the motel.

4

Cal lay in bed. They had left the curtains back and the window cranked open. The light outside was peeling down in stripes and through the window he could feel the night air. Riley was breathing heavy, through the nose. His mouth would fall open next. He would start snoring in a few minutes and then the sleep would get harder.

Cal closed his eyes and thought about the fight. Somewhere in the long second round. His head had been heavy and congested and through the congestion he had felt his own panic. They clinched up in the corner. Rivera got hold of his head and started whaling away. The shots were landing hard and they were landing direct. It felt like his head was getting unscrewed. He reached out and tried to stop him. He could feel his jaw getting slack and his eyes were watering. He felt the panic again, this time right up in his throat. The ref motioned between them to break up the clinch.

They drew apart. He stood in the ring. He closed his

eyes and breathed. His let his head fall back. He looked up and he saw the replay flash across the screens. He saw himself. It wasn't anyone he recognized. He saw him reaching out in panic. He saw him stumbling backward. He saw him closing his eyes to the blows. He didn't look like anything he knew. He was still looking at the screens when the ref restarted the fight. He only snapped his chin back down when he saw Rivera coming at him.

The fight continued. Rivera continued. It took everything Cal had to make it through the third round. There were half a dozen times when Rivera was hair-close to finishing him. Even so, the thought of winning never left him entirely. He kept thinking about the replay. He kept wondering if that was the way it really looked. He didn't feel like a loser until the final bell rang and he realized there was no more time to turn things around. Until then, he had still thought there was time.

After the fight, he couldn't look at Riley. They sat backstage. He leaned on the ice packs taped to his ribs and he closed his eyes and rested. Riley pulled a chair up beside the mat and sat down.

After a few minutes Cal opened his eyes. He stared at the leg of Riley's folding chair. The paint was chipped and the metal was rusted in parts where it showed through. He remembered thinking it was out of place. Everything else in the stadium was so new it was shining.

He said, "I don't know." His breath was still shallow.

Riley nodded. He wasn't looking at Cal. He was leaning forward with his arms resting on his knees as he stared at the floor.

"I guess I was more nervous than I thought."

Riley looked relieved. He stood up. "It happens to everyone. Don't worry about it."

"I just kind of lost it out there."

Riley nodded as he stood above Cal. Cal looked up at him. The light was funny and Riley was just a vague shape as he spoke. He shrugged. He said, "Happened to me once. Went out and choked."

Cal nodded. Riley's head kept moving in and out of shadow. He blinked a couple times but the light didn't change.

"It happen to you too?"

"Sure, kid. Happens to everyone. Go out and act like nobody you know in the ring. Craziest thing." He knelt beside Cal. Gently, he adjusted the ice packs. "You'll be okay. For a minute you had me scared there."

"He was tough."

"Yeah, he's tough. Man—he's tough."

"I didn't expect for him to be so strong."

"Well, we didn't know nothing about him. Didn't even look at the tapes. Stupid or what? We got careless."

"Yeah."

A young boy from the promotion came into the dressing room. He carried his embarrassment flush in front of him as he came in the door. People were always embarrassed around a loser. They didn't know how to act. Cal realized it was the first time it had happened to him, other people's embarrassment. It was his first loss. Up until then all he'd known was the winning. The boy avoided looking at him and went straight up to Riley.

"They want to know if he'll be able to do the postfight interview." He threw his words out abruptly, but Cal was pretty sure it was the nervousness speaking. The kid was clean and polite-looking.

Riley stood up slowly. "Yeah? Who's they? Who's asking?"

The boy turned red. He wet his lips.

Riley shook his head. He jerked his chin at the kid. "Just get the fuck out of here, kid. Before I do I don't know what."

Stuttering, the boy nodded and backed out of the room. The door slammed behind him.

Cal said, "He'll be back." His eyes were closed, but he was smiling.

Riley nodded. "I figure it'll buy you another ten minutes." He looked sheepish.

"You didn't have to give the kid such a hard time."

"Hey, he gets paid a regular salary to get a hard time."

"I guess so."

He was silent as he rested with his eyes closed.

"Hey, Riley."

"What?"

"I'm okay, you know. I'll be okay to do all the press and stuff. You don't have to worry about me."

"I'm not worried."

"I'm okay."

"Get some rest."

Cal was quiet. He felt as if he could sleep. He guessed the painkillers must be working now, because the pain was not so bad that he couldn't see past it. He thought about sleeping and then knew he wouldn't be able to. Not yet. The adrenaline was pushing too hard against the medication. Sleep was still just an idea, but at least now he could see the thought. At least now he could think it. He wondered if he could sit up. If he could sit up, he would be okay for the interview and the walk out from the arena and the bus ride back to the motel with the other fighters. All of that would follow, if he could just sit up.

"Hey Riley."

"What is it, kid?"

"I'm okay. Don't worry about me."

"Shut up."

"I mean it. I'm okay. I don't want for you to worry."

"Just shut up and get some rest." His voice was gentle and now he crouched beside Cal and rested a hand on his shoulder. "You cold?"

Cal shook his head. "No."

"Okay."

It was twenty minutes before the boy was back and by then Cal was sitting in a chair. It had taken the boy three laps around the arena before he found somebody. A man in his fifties, wearing an expensive suit. He walked in first. The boy followed behind him. The man nodded to Riley. He knew Riley. Riley nodded back, ignoring the boy.

"The doctors?"

"Nothing serious," Riley said. "A mashed up eye. A couple stitches to the head. He cleaned up okay." The man nodded.

"I'm ready to do the interviews," Cal said.

"We don't want to force you. But the press are keen to speak with you."

"I'll do the interviews."

He did the interviews. He walked through the first few questions. It was about the third or fourth question. Some guy with a lot of facial hair and bad BO asked it. He leaned forward as he spoke. He leaned real close, holding his tape recorder just in front of Cal's mouth.

"Rivera was the underdog walking in. Were you expecting him to take control of the fight like that?"

For a moment Cal just stared at the recorder. His mind was blank. He cleared his throat and said, "I guess probably I wasn't."

"This is a pretty big loss for you. Speaking for myself, I was surprised by the way you looked in the ring. You never seemed to get into your game. What happened?"

He didn't know what to say. They were waiting for him to respond. He could hear them waiting. He looked up and then he looked at the man asking the question.

"I guess he was just the better guy." He paused. He stared at the man. "I'm sorry. I don't have an explanation. I guess tonight he was just the better guy."

The man from the promotion, the middle-aged man in the expensive suit, appeared at his side. "All right, we have to wrap things up—"

Cal returned to the locker room. He lay back down. He was aching everywhere and he thought he probably should go to the hospital but the question had opened something up inside him. He saw the swing of Rivera's body. He saw the screens overhead and then he heard the guy's voice, asking the questions.

He heard the door open. Riley walked in. He opened his eyes and watched him sit down.

"Hey Riley."

"Yeah?"

He stopped. He rolled his head so he could see Riley. His head was lying flat on the mat and he was looking at Riley sideways.

"Was it really that bad?"

Riley stood up. Cal watched as he walked across the room. He picked up a bag and started packing things in.

"Riley?"

He put the bag down. Cal looked at him, from across the room.

"What, kid?"

"Was it as bad as that guy said? It didn't feel that bad. Was it really that bad?"

Riley shrugged.

"I just want to know."

"I guess it was pretty bad."

Cal closed his eyes. He turned his head and then he opened them again. He stared up at the ceiling.

"Shit happens. It was a tough fight."

"I know."

He closed his eyes.

"Don't take it hard, kid. Don't take it like it means something."

"Sure."

He could hear Riley's footsteps and when he opened his eyes he was kneeling over him.

"We should get you home."

He nodded.

"Come on. Let's get you home."

They went home. Cal sat at home for a week. Normally he would be back in the gym the next day. This time he sat at home. Somebody from the gym came by with the tapes. He didn't touch them. They sat on top of the VCR. He sat on the couch and he thought about the fight.

After a second week Riley stopped by. He banged on the door until Cal came to open it. They looked at each other and then Cal turned and walked back into the house. Riley followed after him.

"What's going on?"

Cal shrugged. He sat down on the couch.

"You gonna sit on your ass forever or what?"

Cal looked up at him. "You want a beer?"

"We need to talk."

"Sure. Sit down."

Riley sat down. He looked at Cal. He leaned forward.

"Okay. It was a bad loss. I'm not gonna pretend otherwise. So what? You learn something from it and you move on. You don't get stuck on it. You don't dwell on it like it means something. You move on."

Cal looked at Riley.

"It's not that simple, is it?"

"Fighting's a pretty simple game."

"It's not that simple."

"Kid, I don't care how simple or not simple it is. I'm talking about getting you off your ass and back into the gym. Rivera's out there and he's saying your name. He's saying you're just about the best fighter he's ever faced. You did good in that fight. Whether you want to admit it or not. There's a lot of good match-ups out there for you still."

Cal didn't say anything. Riley stood up.

"It had to happen sometime. Kid, it happens to everyone. You're not any different."

He looked at Cal. Cal didn't respond. Riley shook his head and walked to the door. He opened it and then he turned and looked back at Cal.

"You're still a hell of a fighter. Maybe you don't want to think you are. I know how that is. I'm looking at you now and I can tell you don't want to think you are. But maybe it's not up to you."

He paused. Then he shook his head again and walked out. The door closed behind him.

Cal heard Riley's car start. He sat and listened to the sound of it disappearing down the drive. He didn't know how to put it. He didn't know how to say it to Riley. At some point the fight with Rivera had become terrifyingly real. It had no semblance to a game. There were no rules or rounds or demarcations, there was no beginning or end. He stood in the middle of the fight. He looked out and it was like he couldn't see where it would end.

Up until then he had only seen one half of the game. He had only seen the winning half. When you stayed in the winning half you could see the game a certain way. When you dropped into the other half the game looked different. It looked real. You saw that you could get hurt. Being in the ring became different after that.

He'd seen the fight for what it really was, and the knowing changed everything. He could no longer pretend it was something simple and finite, something ordered and contained. He could no longer pretend it was something that made sense. He thought about it and he didn't know if he had the stomach for it. He didn't know if he knew how to fight that kind of fight.

He closed his eyes. He remembered what Riley had said. It happened to everyone. It happened and you moved on. Fighting had been the whole of his life. He didn't know anything else. The feeling would have to pass. He would work and he would wait until it passed. He would wait because there was nothing else for him.

He went back into the gym. He went back to training. It was hard. He felt embarrassed just driving up to the place. He got out of the car and he stood outside and he was nervous. He never thought the gym would make him nervous. He stood outside the gym and he had to psych himself up, just to walk through the front doors.

Nothing about the place had changed. It was exactly the same. The guys were exactly the same. They acted like nothing had happened. They asked him questions about Rivera. Rivera was a big star now. They had a lot of questions about Rivera. Cal looked at Riley and Riley looked so relieved to have him back he thought maybe it was going to be okay. He thought if Riley was glad to have him back it had to mean there was somewhere to go. It had to mean there was a way out of this feeling.

Going back was hard. That was one thing. Getting back into the ring was another. They gave him an easy fight. They threw him a fish. Walking out to the ring he was shaking. Riley had to guide him by the shoulder. He stepped into the ring and when they pushed the guard into his mouth he almost threw up. He choked back the bile. He stood in the corner. He looked at the other guy and it was like vertigo got hold of him.

He won the fight, but fighting wasn't easy anymore. Fighting was never easy again. He took some losses. He sat and he waited for his head to get back into the game. He waited fight after fight and then it hit him how long he'd been waiting. It hit him, how far away the game had gone. He saw it for the first time and he was bewildered by it. That the whole thing could be so fragile. That it could fall away so quick.

He started to think maybe he'd never fight top-tier competition again. The thought was terrible, but there was a relief in it. Something that was formerly impossible became the only thing that made sense. He thought it made a lot of sense. He thought he was being realistic about his chances.

He got used to the idea, so that when the news came it was the last thing he expected. He went to the gym one day and there was something in Riley's face. He pulled Cal to one side.

"We got a rematch."

For a second Cal wasn't sure what he was talking about. Then it came to him, slowly.

"Rivera?"

"Rivera."

"Huh."

He couldn't grasp it. He stood and he tried to think what it meant. The idea of facing Rivera had slipped away from him. It was a difficult thing to imagine. It had been four years but it felt much longer. He couldn't remember the fighter he'd been four years ago. He couldn't remember the fighter Rivera wanted to rematch. He realized

Riley was waiting for him to say something. He cleared his throat.

"What do you think?"

"I think you got a chance. I think you got more than a chance."

He turned and looked at Riley. The excitement was plain in his face. He was trying not to show it. But Cal could see it. Cal knew Riley pretty well. Enough to read him. He kept looking at him.

"You figure?"

"Yeah. I figure."

Cal turned and stared straight ahead. He could feel Riley looking up at him. Maybe Riley was right. Maybe he had a chance, and maybe it wasn't over the way he'd thought. He turned and looked at Riley and he saw the feeling in his eyes again. He looked at him and no didn't seem right. He shook his head.

"Okay."

"Yeah?"

"Yeah."

Riley exhaled. He grinned at Cal. "They'll schedule it in the next few months. I think we got enough time. We got a lot of work to do, but I think we got enough time."

Cal turned away. He thought about the fight and he thought about Rivera and it was like something came alive. Not inside him. But all around him. Maybe Riley was right. Maybe it was what he had been waiting for. The fight could change things. Nobody could say it couldn't change things. Nobody could say that it wouldn't.

He and Riley started training. They trained, and he felt the fight growing in his body. His head was clear for the first time in years. He thought that must be because of the fight. He found himself looking forward to it. He found himself thinking about it all the time. The promoter fixed the date. The fight was confirmed and the contracts signed. He looked at Riley. He could see how he was pleased.

He thought about the first fight. He remembered that he'd been close. He'd been closer than people knew. There had been moments when it could have gone either way. He'd almost forgotten that. Now he remembered. He remembered it daily. There were things people didn't know. Things he'd almost forgotten.

Cal lay in bed. He closed his eyes, and then he slept for ten hours.

5

The next morning Cal went out for his run, same as the day before. He went early to avoid the heat. It was only eight but already the air was thicker and he could see the smog coming off the city as he peeled down the empty streets. Now and again he heard a car idle in some side street and then kick into gear. There were no birds to speak of. He hadn't noticed it the day before, but there were no birds to speak of, anywhere in this town.

The city was *flat*. There was hardly a bump in the sidewalk, just flat running off in every direction. It made the run easy. His feet pounded the pavement. He tried to keep his pace even but it kept creeping up and pretty soon he gave in to it. He turned the corner, flying. The city stayed flat no matter how fast he ran. It was like he could run forever and still never reach the hills. He wondered how people kept from going crazy in this town. He wondered how they kept from running off in one direction and never turning back again.

He checked the bounce in his gait, checked his pace again. He didn't want to let the boredom get the better of him.

He ran the same course as yesterday. He was in good condition and breathing light the whole way, and that despite the pace. He moved fast and he moved easy, like it wasn't just for recreation and health. Still, he'd never pass for a runner. In the ring he was pretty quick on his feet, but put him out to run and he'd always look like he was lumbering, no matter how fast he moved. It didn't bother him. Anyway he didn't run for speed and he didn't move for grace. He used to build his cardio on the mat, but as he got older it took more to keep it up. He had to add to the routine. Add in circuits on the bike and reps on the machines. Add in daily runs. He didn't mind it so much. He didn't hate it.

He sprinted the last five minutes. He sprinted so that his breathing would be shallow and his chest heaving and the sweat flying off him like a crown. He sprinted straight up to the motel, arms pumping, down the flat sidewalk, and when he got there he came to a stop and doubled over for a second and then straightened up again immediately to get the air back into his lungs. He walked around the block, breathing noisily. The street was quiet and the breathing was loud in his head. Cal smiled to himself. He sounded like a goddamned horse.

Riley said he'd meet him at the restaurant for breakfast. The motel was quiet when he entered. He craned his neck to read the clock hanging behind the front desk. The manager wasn't there but the clock read past eight and he still couldn't hear a thing. It didn't seem like there was anyone else even staying in the place. He thought for a second about Riley and the manager and he shook his head. He headed up to the room and showered quickly to get off the sweat. Then he headed next door to eat.

When he walked into the diner, Riley was sitting at a back booth reading the paper. He was wearing his glasses but he was still squinting at the pages. He was squinting hard, like he had something against the news he was reading. Cal slid in across the table from him.

Riley looked up. The squint softened. "Coffee?"

Cal shook his head. "Just some juice."

Riley nodded and waved at a passing waitress. She slowed by their table. She parked her coffee pot on the edge of the table. She looked at Riley.

"Some juice," Riley said. He looked at Cal. "Orange? Or what?"

"Yeah. Some orange juice would be great. And water."

The waitress nodded. "Okay. And I'll send your server over to take your order."

Riley folded the paper and cleared his throat. "How you feeling? You sleep okay?"

"Yeah, okay." Cal looked around the table.

"What you looking for? The menu?" Riley handed it to him. Cal flipped through the breakfast pages, reading slow.

"You order?"

"Nah. Just been drinking coffee and having a look at the paper."

"Oh."

"Hungry?"

"Pretty hungry."

He continued studying the menu. He looked up at Riley. His forehead wrinkled up. His eyes smiled.

"What?"

"Those glasses make me laugh."

Riley reached up. Carefully, he pulled them off and folded them. "The doctor said I need them for reading small things," he said. He placed them in his shirt pocket and then patted the pocket.

Cal was back to studying the menu.

"How was your run?"

"Good."

"You know what you want?"

He nodded. Riley looked up. A waitress was coming their way with the orange juice and water. She was American, and younger than the other waitresses by maybe two or three years. It was getting so those years didn't count for much. She placed the juice in front of Cal and the water in front of Riley. She didn't blink when Riley slid the water back to Cal's side.

"You boys ready to order?" Her voice was low and the words rattled around in it.

"Yeah. And I could use a refill on the coffee," Riley said.

The waitress nodded. "Uh-huh." She took out a pad of paper and plucked a pencil out from her hairdo. The hairdo stayed in place. "Okay. Go ahead." She looked at Cal.

"I'll have the breakfast platter."

"One breakfast platter. You want your eggs scrambled, boiled or fried?"

"Fried."

"You want bacon, ham or sausage links?"

"Sausage."

"You want beans, hash browns or breakfast potatoes?"

"Potatoes."

"You want tortillas? Or you want toast, you want brown or white toast?"

Cal hesitated. "Brown."

She nodded as she wrote the order down. She smiled at Cal through her lipstick.

"That was pretty good. I like a guy who knows what he wants."

Cal was looking at the menu and frowning. He looked up at her.

"Can I have an order of pancakes to go with that?"

"Hungry, huh?" She made eyes at Cal. She played with her pencil, tapping out a dance against her shirtfront. He looked down. He folded his hands on the table. He concentrated on his hands, knuckle by knuckle.

Riley cleared his throat. "I'll just have scrambled eggs with bacon. And white toast." He snapped the menu shut. The waitress wrote the order down without looking up.

She shoved the pencil back into her hair and tucked the pad into the front of her apron.

Riley paused. "And how about that coffee?"

The waitress nodded. She slipped her eyes to Riley and then back over to Cal as she leaned over to pick up their menus. They watched her fingers brush along the tabletop. She looked at them and smiled.

"Okay, boys. Coming right up." She dipped as she turned and walked away slow.

Cal stretched his back out. "I didn't know the breakfast platter came with that many questions. I might not have ordered it if I'd known it came with that many questions."

"You looked like you panicked on brown toast."

"Yeah. I guess I did." Cal laughed. He nodded at the paper. "So, what's new in the world?"

Riley shoved it to one side. "Nothing much."

"Okay."

"That waitress is checking you out."

"What?" Cal twisted round a little in his chair.

"I said, that waitress is checking you out. Still is."

Cal frowned and turned back into his seat.

"Not your type?"

"I don't have a type."

"Too bad for her. She looks smitten." Cal didn't respond. Riley grunted. "I just hope she doesn't screw our order up. She was too busy flirting to pay attention."

"She wrote it all down."

"Sure," Riley said. "I guess she did."

Cal drank his orange juice. Riley waited for his coffee.

"She's still checking you—"

"Jesus Christ, Riley."

The waitress returned carrying the coffee pot. Conversation died. She killed it just walking over. She smiled at Cal. She smiled at Riley. They were careful to ignore her. The woman didn't need encouraging. She refilled Riley's coffee. She brought Cal another orange juice. She brought cutlery and napkins and rearranged the salt and pepper shakers and brought them fresh water and then she gave up and left. Cal exhaled.

"This sure is a weird town."

"Yeah, well. You get used to it."

"You end up in some funny spots—"

"It takes you places."

"Sure does."

Riley sighed. He craned his neck and looked at the waitress. She was popping bubble gum and staring off into space. Her eyes were glazed and the sunlight was hitting her hard in the face. He turned back and looked at Cal.

"I guess that's TJ for you."

Cal smiled.

"Did you just call it TJ?"

"What?"

"You just called it TJ."

"Course I did. Everybody calls it TJ."

"Who calls it TJ?"

"Everybody."

"Come on."

"Yeah, sure they do. Just like they call Dago, Dago. TJ. It's TJ."

"Bullshit."

"It's kind of like LA. Or SF."

"Nobody calls it SF. I guess maybe sometimes they call it Frisco."

"I'm just saying. You listen up and you'll see that everyone is calling it TJ."

Cal was still smiling.

"Fuck off."

Their food arrived. The waitress brought it on a giant tray that she balanced on one hand and she slid it onto the table, plate by plate. The table was covered in dishes and steam came up off their eggs. There was an extra portion of bacon for Cal. The waitress winked at him. Her eye fluttered unsteadily, caked with shadow and mascara. He looked up at her and nodded politely. He smiled, a little, then looked down again. She left them with their food.

Cal shook salt and pepper onto his eggs. He spread a little butter onto his toast. The toast was hot so that the butter melted fast. He pulled an egg onto the toast using two fingers and then he cut into the yolk with his knife so that it ran down the edges of the toast and mixed with the butter. He took a bite. While he was chewing, he dropped maple syrup onto the pancakes and then he cut into that, alternating with bites of sausage.

They ate steadily and without talking and when they

were done they pushed their plates away and leaned back into their seats. Cal looked at Riley. Riley sipped his coffee and looked back at him.

"What time's the weigh-in again?"

"Three. They got press coming to that."

"They got press down here?"

"Come on."

"I'm kidding."

"They paid a lot for you guys. They need to get their money's worth and they need to get their inches. Just like anybody else."

"Any of the guys down here?"

"Sure. A couple places sent their boys."

"You run into them?"

"Yeah."

"I've not seen anybody."

"You've been going to bed early. Sleeping all day. It's good."

Cal nodded. He yawned.

"You think Rivera's in town already?"

"Probably."

"It's so quiet, you wouldn't think there was a fight on tomorrow."

"You know how it is. They'll all just flood in last minute."

"You seen him?"

Riley shook his head. "I saw Murilo."

"Oh."

"Yeah."

"That means Rivera's got to be around somewhere."

"Uh-huh. Murilo doesn't stray too far from his boy."

"How was he?"

"Who? Murilo?" Riley shrugged. "I don't know. He looked older."

"He is older."

"Aren't we all."

"You hear any news on what kind of weight Rivera's making?"

"I hear he's walking around at 220." He paused. "He won't have any trouble making weight, if that's what you're thinking."

Cal nodded. He looked at the spare plate of bacon.

"Will you eat the bacon?"

"Just leave it."

"I don't want to hurt her feelings and I don't like bacon. Will you eat it?"

Riley shrugged. He leaned over and picked up a few rashers with his fingers. He ate them, chewing noisily. He wiped his fingers on a napkin as he swallowed.

"Good enough?"

"Let's go."

Riley nodded. Cal shook out a couple of bills onto the table. They stood up and walked out of the restaurant. The waitress looked after them and then she sighed and started clearing their table. She counted over the bills before sliding them into her apron pocket.

They stood outside.

"What's the time?"

"I don't know. Somewhere around nine I guess."

"I want to stop by the Caliente. See how they're getting on."

Cal shrugged. "Okay."

"We got time. It's down this way."

They turned and walked down the street. Cal was staring down at the pavement as they walked. He looked like he was concentrating on his feet, on moving one and then the other and then the next. Riley couldn't tell what he was thinking. He looked sideways into his eyes and maybe it was just the angle and the light, but they looked clouded up to him.

"You feeling okay?"

"I feel fine."

"You don't want to be overdoing it."

"I went easy on the run."

"Okay."

The street was quiet and the sun was now very bright and it still didn't feel like there was a fight on the next night. They kept walking down the street. They watched the pedestrians crossing the roads. The shoeshine boys had deserted their posts and were crouching in the shade. They joked with each other, their voices carrying in the heat. Riley looked at them and frowned. He cleared his throat.

"So I showed a couple of your old fights at that clinic I did in San Pedro."

"Which ones?" Cal's voice was disinterested.

"Hansen. Daniels."

"Oh."

"Shit, man. You were beautiful back then. You remember?"

"I remember."

"You *plowed* through those guys."

Cal shrugged. They both fell silent. They continued walking and soon they came up on the Caliente. Cal looked at it. The place was sitting in the middle of a gravel lot. He guessed it was for parking. It looked like it could park a lot of cars. The building looked pretty big. They used it for concerts and they used it for parties and once a month or so they used it for fights. He'd heard they packed it out with locals and tourists from across the border. He guessed they would get together a pretty good crowd.

From the outside it didn't look too different from a normal sporting stadium. It had the same blocky concrete and the same matter-of-fact gray and from the ramps running down the side it looked like it opened up underground. There were consignment vans jamming the parking lot and workers carrying in metal rods and curtaining and anyway it wasn't what Cal had been expecting. Outside, posters advertised the fights and through the front doors the lobby area looked pretty spacious.

The posters had big font and cut-out pictures of him and Rivera. They were old promo shots. Over the years the photos had circulated pretty freely and he was used to looking at both of them. He looked at them again. Rivera looked pretty silly with his fists clenched together and his mouth drawn down like a monkey. He guessed he didn't look much better with that vacant expression and his arms folded high across his chest. It was funny to see the photos placed side by side like that. It was funny seeing himself next to Rivera again.

He looked at the poster, uneasily. They had skewed the perspective so he looked the same size and bulk as Rivera. Maybe even a little bit bigger. They had overcompensated.

Riley came up beside him. He looked at the posters.

"They're all over town."

"Town—for me that's the street between the motel and the warehouse."

"Bet it feels good to be headlining again."

Cal nodded. Riley jerked his head toward the building.

"Let's go in and take a look."

They walked around to the back and slipped in through a side door. Riley was whistling as they walked down a long fluorescent-lit corridor. The air-conditioning was blasting through the building and the corridor was empty. Their footsteps echoed as they walked. They saw a door leading into the main hall and took it.

It was even colder in the hall. The place was just a massive shell. The floor was concrete and the rafters were exposed and above the rafters the roof was sheets of tin paneling. The place was big. They were setting up bleacher seats and lighting rigs and laying down long swaths of black cloth so it would look bigger. The place would clean up good. Cal could already tell it would clean up good.

Riley walked forward into the hall.

"Watch your feet."

Cal nodded. The floor was covered in cables and they moved as the men worked. There were about a dozen people rushing around, shouting out instructions in Spanish and calling for stops and starts of the rigging. Overhead screens were hanging down from the ceiling and it looked like they were setting up a stage at the front. The stage was flanked with enormous speakers and there was a walkway running to the center of the floor. They didn't have the ring up yet. There was just an empty space in the middle where the ring would go.

Cal looked around. He looked at the people. It was funny to think it had to do with him. Watching it like this it didn't seem to have anything to do with him, but already it had made the idea of the fight more real. He could feel it getting more real as he stood there. He swallowed and rolled out his neck and turned to look for Riley.

"I thought maybe they'd have the ring up," Riley said. "I thought maybe they'd have it up by now."

"They got a day. More than a day."

"I was hoping they'd want it up for the press conference but I guess not," Riley said. He had his shoulders hunched up.

Cal looked around him again. He looked at the lights. He looked at the speakers. He looked at the yard-high walkways and the metal railings for keeping the fans off and then he rolled out his neck again.

"Pretty big production."

"Yeah. They put on a good show. I guess they got money coming in from somewhere. Television money maybe."

They walked back the same way they had come, stepping over cables and keeping out of the way of the workers. They dropped into the fluorescent-lit corridor, double-tracking their way back.

A woman turned the corner, walking briskly. Her face was tense and she was talking emphatically into her cell phone but when she saw them her face loosened up. Like magic it loosened. She waved and stopped. Riley stopped too. Abruptly, she ended her telephone conversation. She turned to them, smiling.

"Josie—you've met Cal before I guess."

"Years back." She put out her hand. Cal shook it. He couldn't remember meeting her. She beamed at him. "You guys taking a look around?"

"Yeah. I was hoping maybe the ring would be up."

"They should have it up by the afternoon."

Riley jerked his head in the direction of the hall. "It looks good."

"It's getting there."

"How many does it seat?"

"Little over four thousand. I don't know how they get all those seats in there, but somehow they do."

"You doing the press stuff in there?"

"No, it's too dark and loud—we use a place around the corner. You guys got the information for that?"

Riley nodded. "Yeah, somewhere. I got it written down." He jabbed his chin toward Josie. "You know if Rivera's around?"

"He's around. I saw him yesterday. He's having a public training session in a bit. I'm just about to head over."

"A public training session? The day before the fight?" Riley kept his voice casual. Cal looked at him.

Josie shrugged. "I don't know how much of a session it'll actually be. But he wanted the press there, and the press aren't hanging around Tijuana for more than a day or two. We talked it back and forth and in the end he gave in and scheduled it for this morning."

"He holding it around here?"

Josie nodded. "Across the border in San Diego. At his new place."

"What new place?"

"He's just opened up a gym."

"In San Diego?"

"Yeah. He's holding the session at 10:30, and then he'll head down here, bringing all the press with him. We've got a bus picking them up. We'll bring them down and feed them lunch and send them straight into the weigh-ins."

"Make sure they don't wander off." Riley smiled.

"Yeah. For some reason people tend to get lost in Tijuana." She laughed. "Rivera's training session could be interesting. I'm hoping it is. He's got some new guys that he's pushing hard. We've got a couple of them on the card tomorrow."

"Whereabouts he open his place?"

"You know San Diego?"

"Sure, a bit. Done a couple of guest spots there."

"It's just around the corner from Frank's place, on Delaney."

"Oh yeah, I know it. Nice area." Riley paused. "So Rivera's moving up stateside."

The woman Josie shook her head. "Don't think so. I'm pretty sure it's just a gym with his name attached to it. I don't know the ins and outs of the arrangement exactly, but it's something like that."

"Interesting."

"He's been smart, Rivera. He's done well with his money."

"Well, you're not doing so bad yourself." Riley grinned and patted her on the shoulder.

"We're trying." She was smiling back and then her phone started ringing again. She looked down at the phone, then flipped it open. "I better take this—" Her voice was apologetic.

"No problem. We'll let ourselves out," Riley said. She nodded. She held out her hand to Cal. He looked at her.

She was mouthing good-bye and saying hello into the telephone and shaking his hand, all at the same time. Cal smiled. They walked off in opposite directions.

"Nice lady."

"She's great, Josie. A real hard-ass when it comes to business, but great. She's been a fan of yours a long time."

"I don't remember meeting her."

"No," Riley said. "You wouldn't."

They walked outside.

"What's the time?"

"Ten."

"Okay."

They were silent. Riley was walking fast as they headed back in the direction of the motel. Cal nodded to him.

"You going?"

"Of course I'm going."

Cal nodded, to himself. He looked across the street. He could see posters hanging in store windows and pasted up on walls. Riley was right. They were everywhere. He wondered how he had missed them before.

"You're right," he said to Riley. "They got those posters up everywhere."

"Yeah."

They had reached the motel. Riley jerked his head in the direction of the parking lot.

"I'd better be heading off. It might take a little time crossing the border."

"Okay."

Riley nodded. He shoved his hands into his pockets. He felt inside them to make sure he had the car keys.

"You got the room key?"

Cal said, "It'll be okay."

"What?"

"I said, it'll be okay."

"Sure it'll be okay. I'm just wondering how he's going to look. I was just thinking about it."

"He'll look the way he'll look."

"What are you going to do?"

"Take it easy. I don't know. There's nothing to do."

"It's the day before the fight."

"I know."

"Just get some rest. You've got the weigh-ins and the press stuff later. It'll be a circus."

"It always is."

"I better get going."

"Okay."

Riley nodded, one last time. Then he headed in the direction of the car. Cal stood and watched as he climbed into the Jeep. He raised a hand and kept watching as Riley swung out of the lot. He was driving in a hurry and barely raised his hand in reply as he turned down the road. Cal turned and trudged up the stairs to their room.

6

Riley drove down the freeway, fast. He'd slipped right over the border. From the border it was only fifteen minutes to San Diego. If he concentrated and got his directions straight, he would get there on time, or pretty close to it. He was agitated and he knew it. The feeling was hard in his stomach so that all the calm of the past few days disappeared. He didn't need for the feeling to show. He would need all the proving of his usual, braying confidence, walking into Rivera's place.

He flipped on the radio—an old reflex. *"La major musica juvenil del momento, pop, rock, electronica—"* The radio blurted out words, like it was in a hurry too. He slammed his fist onto the dashboard. The car rattled a little but the speakers kept dumping words at him. Furious, he jabbed at the controls. He went harder than he meant. The dial came off between his fingers. "Cheap mother-fucking piece of *shit*—" He threw it against the window. It bounced back at him, hard, and fell to the floor.

He had a bad feeling. The whole situation smelled *bad*. He felt like he was driving into a trap. He felt it like it was right here in the car with him, like it was riding shotgun. He'd been concentrating too hard on Cal. Hiding out in bumfuck Tijuana, studying the kid's game, getting all excited because he'd picked up a few new tricks. Christ. Thinking so hard he almost forgot about Rivera. Now all of a sudden it was like Rivera was all he could see. That was the price. The man was everywhere inside his head. Up in between his eyes, blurring up his vision like a fucking migraine.

Breathing deep, Riley laid out facts. He tried to place it. It was in the way Josie had spoken. It was in the new gym, opening up stateside, across the border and legit. It was in the bus, scheduled to pick up the press—they were expecting a busload of press to turn up. It was in the fact of *him* driving *now*, speeding, frantic, just to catch a glimpse of him.

He never saw a man who looked so much like a nightmare. Pale, hairless, too big and bulked up to be a lightheavy. His lips were thick and protruding and he held his mouth half open so the corners didn't meet right. Spittle would collect there, once he got older. His eyes were large and staring and the pupils always showed very small and very black. There was no fair trade in his gaze. He looked right into you, through those pale eyes, from under that bricked-up forehead, but when you looked back at him his eyes were flat and opaque and there was nothing to see.

He never changed. He heard Cal's voice—*he recovers fast; he's back in the game before you can do anything.* That was the thing about Rivera. He always came back. He always returned. Staring through those blank eyes and those straight uncurling lashes. Carrying his mouth propped open and his breath coming heavy. It was obscene. Everything about him was obscene. Riley felt the urge to slam on the brakes and to fight the feeling he pressed his foot onto the gas and dialed the car down the highway so fast he thought he heard sirens ringing in his ear.

He made San Diego in twenty minutes. He was surprised Border Patrol hadn't collared him for a stop. A big car, speeding down the freeway, just across the border—he guessed it was his lucky day. He laughed grimly and concentrated on his exits. He turned his corners neat and once he was in the neighborhood he just drove around looking for the crowd. He looked for the cars, figuring he'd recognize some of them. Ranallo's old white Honda—it jumped out at him. His eye ticked over the street. He saw Smithson's new Jeep. Barney's Lexus. Woody's piece-of-shit Toyota. He saw the bus chartered by the TFL, ready to round them up. It was a *big* bus. He was in the right place.

Outside, everything was quiet. The parking lot was full and the streets were choked up with cars but he didn't see so much as a passerby. The building was big and barren and on the outside they had tinkered up some letters spelling SÃO PAULO TOP TEAM. It couldn't be called fancy, but real estate was starting to come at a premium in this neighborhood. He figured the address was doing the kind of work no amount of paint and frills was going to do. He drove by once to check it out and then two more times looking for parking. He found a space on a side street around the corner. He squeezed the car in and then he got out and hurried over toward the gym.

He didn't slow his pace right up to the building. He opened the door. The place was packed. It was buzzing. Journalists leaned up against the back wall, clicking at tape recorders. Tripods set with digital cameras were skewed up in a line. Riley craned his neck to look around.

Before he looked for faces, he checked out Rivera's digs. The place was big. There were three rings. Three! Down one end of the room there were leather bags, all brand new. There were mats for grappling. The main room broke off into two smaller spaces at the back. One was full of weights and machines. The other looked like a second practice space for sparring. There was a row of doors down one side of the main room. He counted them off—storage, office, locker room. He craned his neck. He couldn't be sure, but it looked like the last door was a sauna. The wood doors and the little glass window sure looked like it. The envy hit him hard. State of the art. Rivera's place was fucking state of the art.

"Riley, my man."

He looked over.

"Yann."

"Didn't expect to see you here."

"Didn't you?"

"Maybe I did."

They smiled at each other. Riley felt himself relax, a notch. Yann was safe. Yann was family. Riley went over and stood next to him. He was leaning with one foot propped against the wall and now he folded his arms across his chest and nodded to Riley. He was a couple inches taller than Riley. On another man those inches would have driven Riley crazy, but on Yann, it just made him seem more safe. On Yann, he liked those inches.

"How's Cal?"

"Good."

"That on record?"

"Sure it is."

"He still knocking people out in practice?"

"Can't stop the kid."

"Never could."

"He'll be happy to see you," Riley said.

"I'll be happy to see him."

Riley jerked his head toward the crowd. "So what's going on here?"

Yann shrugged. "I think it's a no-show."

The words hit him hard. He swallowed.

"No Rivera?" Riley kept his voice even.

Yann shrugged again. "Where you coming from? You down in Tijuana already?"

"I was in the neighborhood."

Yann smiled. Riley stared straight ahead, into the crowd. He cleared his throat.

"So you're sure it's a no-show?"

"He's not showing."

"How long you been waiting?"

"Been here since ten."

"These things always run a bit late."

Yann laughed.

"I keep seeing TFL people running around. They're not saying anything to us, though. They're too busy looking stressed."

He paused. He looked down at Riley. "It's a no-show."

"So why are you all sticking around?"

Yann winked at Riley. "Just in case he shows up."

"Screw you."

"Sorry. It's just your face was pretty funny there for a second."

Riley shook his head. "I knew there wasn't any way Rivera was going to fuck around with a training session the day before a fight."

"He's got his kids turning up in his place."

"Fuck that."

"Yeah."

"So why are you guys sticking around?"

Yann shrugged. "We gotta take some bus down to the border."

"Where's Josie?"

"She's running around somewhere, apologizing to everyone. You'll see her. She looks like hell."

"Why don't you get her to take you guys down now?"

"May as well see the kids. Now that we're here. It's always interesting to see who Rivera's pushing. I'm guessing a few of them are worth checking out."

Riley nodded.

"Riley."

He looked up.

"Spence."

"Good to see you, man."

"I missed you the other week in Vegas."

"Couldn't make it. Family stuff."

"You missed some good fights."

"I heard."

They nodded to each other. He went back to his place in the row of journalists, behind the cameras. Riley looked at Yann.

"So there's a lot of guys here."

"Uh-huh."

"More than I expected."

"It's a good story. Everybody knows Cal was his toughest fight."

"I guess he was."

"I would've killed to see this fight three years ago." Yann smiled. He shook his head. His voice went whimsical. "They wait too long with the rematches nowadays. They let the fire go right out on them."

Riley frowned.

"Tell me about the kids we're going to see."

"Don't know. They haven't told us much." He paused. "I saw one of Murilo's lightweights at those fights in Columbus. Some kid called Cuevas. He looked good."

"How'd he fight?"

"Like they all do."

"Yeah. They're minis. Mini-Riveras."

"They're good."

"I know. But Murilo's always looking for his next Rivera, and it shows in his fighters."

"Sure, Riley. I guess that's true."

They were both silent. Riley fidgeted. "I'm gonna find out what's going on."

Yann shrugged.

"Good luck."

Riley nodded over his shoulder. He moved out from the corner where they had been standing. He skirted the row of cameras, recognizing faces.

"Riley."

"Charlie. You're looking good."

"I've been working on losing this weight."

"I can tell. Almost didn't recognize you there for a minute."

"I got another twenty pounds I gotta lose."

"Well, don't overdo it."

"Hey, Riley, good to see you. Didn't expect you here."

"You know me. Always walking right into the lion's den."

"I guess you heard Rivera's not showing. Fucking piece of shit! I should be asleep in my bed right now."

"Yeah—"

"Riley."

"Tom. How's it kicking?"

"Not too bad. How's Cal?"

"He's good. He's real good."

"Yeah, I heard he's looking good. He gonna give Rivera a fight?"

"Boys, he's gonna *make* the fight."

They laughed. Riley moved down the row. He knew these guys. He'd known them for years. They were jovial and bored and their cheerfulness was doing him good. The shock of Rivera's nonappearance was turning into disappointment, and he was honest enough with himself to admit there was relief cutting against the disappointment.

He didn't stop to think about the relief. That way he wouldn't enjoy it too much. He knew it wasn't going to last. He whipped his head round. He caught sight of Josie.

"Josie."

"Riley. I didn't expect to see you here."

"Well, I felt like a drive."

"I guess you heard?"

"It's a shame, Josie. After you went to all the trouble of organizing things."

"That's life."

"That's tough, you mean. Though I know you're not the type to complain." He nodded at the crowd. "Good turnout."

"I'm just glad people are staying."

"When do you think we'll be starting?"

"Any minute now. And then I want to get people out of here as fast as possible. They've waited long enough."

"So where is Rivera?"

Josie shrugged. "God knows. I guess somewhere down in Tijuana. I just hope he turns up for the weigh-in."

Riley patted her on the shoulder. "He'll turn up. He's a professional, Josie."

She looked up. She nodded at somebody. "They're ready. I have to go," she said. He nodded as she headed off.

Riley picked his way through the crowd back to Yann.

"Any news?"

"She said they'll be starting any minute now."

"What Josie says goes."

"Yeah."

Yann leaned back against the wall. He tilted his head back and watched the floor. A door swung open at the back. The reporters quit their talk and the room settled down. It was a practiced kind of settling. A couple seconds and the cameras would start whirring. Already you could see the elbows working. Riley couldn't see too well over all the heads and tripods. He stepped onto a chair. Now he was too high, sticking out like a sore thumb, but at least he could see. There was Murilo and some of the other trainers from Top Team. There were four fighters, all young. All big.

Riley studied them. He watched the cameras being trained on them. They started whirring just a second earlier than he expected. He didn't blame them. The kids looked good, just standing there. They carried their weight clean. Riley eyeballed them at a couple inches over six feet. Two twenty, 225, give or take. They stood quiet and looked around the room. They looked at the cameras. They waited. They seemed nervous and relaxed at the same time, and that was a good thing. Riley liked the look of them. He liked the look of them a lot.

"What do these kids fight at?" Riley asked Yann.

"Light-heavy. One of them's a welter, believe it or not."

"They're big."

"I guess they cut."

"They look good."

"Yeah."

They started, immediately. Murilo and the other trainers held focus mitts. They paired off—four pairs. They spaced out cautiously. The trainers held the mitts up.

Instantly the floor was crawling with movement. The four fighters moved fast. They leaped up. They circled. They *moved*. They moved clear across the mats, from one side to the other, avoiding collisions, maintaining form. From where Riley was standing, up on the chair, it looked like some kind of demented square dance party. Their rhythm was perfect and the whole time they worked the mitts they worked them quick and hard and fearsome. They threw knees, they threw combinations. They weaved. They worked without break or pause and they didn't need to catch their breath. Their concentration was solid. Riley could see it in their eyes. He could hear it in the noise of glove hitting mitt. He sucked his breath in. Beside him, Yann was nodding, slowly.

They worked for five minutes, then stopped. Admiration was clouding up the room. All four fighters were breathing light and they were smiling at each other as they walked over to strap on shinguards and ankle braces. They had relaxed a little. One of them said something, eyes crinkling up as he smiled. Riley caught the sound of his voice from the back of the room. It was high and untempered. Riley blinked. They were just *kids*. Another one stretched his arms up in the air, idly.

"Ain't youth a beautiful thing," Yann said.

Riley nodded, distracted. "Sure," he said. "Sure."

He had clocked one of the kids, early. The kid with the high voice. He watched him closely. He was quiet and Riley could feel his focus from across the room, but at the same time he seemed happy and relaxed. He looked a little younger than the others. They treated him that way. They chatted and cracked jokes and he nodded, happily. He bobbed his head up and down and his grin was wide and easy.

Murilo organized them for sparring. He picked one of

the bigger kids and he picked the kid with the high voice. Riley's kid. Riley watched the way Murilo talked to them. He watched the way he looked at them. He guessed these two were the ones. He leaned back into the wall, measuring them up. He put them at a couple years apart. Both still in their early twenties. They looked a lot alike, but Riley could pick out differences.

The others cleared the floor. They stood *way* back. Murilo nodded to the two set to spar. They sprang forward. They launched flying knees, spinning back-fists, capoiera kicks. They buzzed with energy. Murilo called out to them. They settled down a bit. They began working their bread and butter. They threw combinations, they threw knees from the clinch.

Their stand-up was hard and flashy. Riley focused. He got past the flashiness. He got into the fundamentals of their game.

The older kid had a reach advantage. It looked like he had the weight advantage too. But Riley had a feeling the younger kid was the one with knockout power. It was just a hunch. They both hit precise, but on the younger kid the striking came fast and it looked reckless. The punch that got you was the one you didn't see coming, and this kid took his game in so many different directions it was hard to see what was coming next. His game was unpredictable, and that could be exploited for big wins in the ring.

Riley kept watching him. He was reading the older kid real good. He was blocking strikes before they were thrown and he never took his eyes from his face. He threw some good combinations. The last one ended with a knee that hit the other kid square. It hurt him; Riley could see it in his face. The older kid moved into the clinch and went for the takedown.

The older kid got the takedown on pure muscle. The younger kid scooted out from under. A slippery, wriggling movement. He was barely half out when he started working submissions. Riley counted four submission attempts in less than sixty seconds. *Four.* The kid with the takedown had good defenses. He slipped out of all four submissions. The other kid pressed on, relentless.

Riley watched him work. There were submissions in there he didn't hardly know the names of, and he was a ground guy. The kid was inventing stuff as he went. People weren't going to know the defenses for these submissions. People weren't going to know what to do against this kind of ground assault. People were going to tap out of sheer bewilderment.

He blinked. Rivera never had submissions like that. Rivera never loved the ground like that.

Murilo shouted something to the fighters. They broke and scrambled back to their feet. They launched back at each other immediately. He could have watched the younger kid's ground game all day, but he guessed he understood Murilo's point. The older kid didn't have the ground game of the younger one. Another thirty seconds and the kid would have caught him. They were more even on their feet. It was more of a fight that way. Besides, it was standing that Rivera's influence best showed. He guessed there was more than one thing going on in this training session.

On their feet, the two fighters flowed very strong and they hit each other hard and once or twice he thought one or the other was rocked, but they still kept going. He watched closely. They went stronger *after* they were rocked. The kids had heart. Both of them.

They were very young and so they fought a ten-minute round without slowing. Toward the end of the round, the older fighter dropped the younger kid to the mat. A nice, tricky move, a clinch that turned into a hard left hook. The younger kid walked right into it. He fell to the mat, eyes alert, already blocking. He didn't look dazed but he was falling. The older kid sprang forward and unleashed the trademark Rivera headstomps. The younger fighter warded them off with his forearms. He swung upkicks. Still, there was a little panic in his face as the older fighter continued with the stomps, foot landing hard and flush. Murilo shouted and they stopped.

The younger fighter sprang to his feet immediately. He was a little dinged around the head. He looked discouraged. He was shaking his head and he had his hands on his hips and he was talking fast in that funny, high voice of his. The other kid threw an arm around his shoulder and he stopped talking. He was still shaking his head though. They walked off the mat together, breathing heavy.

Riley watched them. The older kid had proved stronger, but he would put his money on the younger kid. Nine times out of ten he would put his money on the younger kid. He'd bet the kid was only twenty-two, twenty-three. Give him another year or two and he'd be sweeping up belts. *All* the belts. He'd be plucking them from three-time champions. He'd be robbing veterans. He'd knock contenders into early retirement—they'd lose heart, just watching him warm up. A kid like this could change the fight game for good.

Riley didn't take his eyes off him. He was already breathing normal and he was moving easy. He would have been good for another two rounds. He watched Murilo clap him on the shoulder before directing the remaining two fighters to the floor. He watched the way he looked into his eyes.

The other kids started sparring. They were pretty impressive too. They didn't have the physical abilities of the first two, but they fought smart and they fought canny. They reminded him of Rivera. They tricked each other out. They laid traps for each other. They feinted, they faked. Everything looked hard and calculated and if their game lacked the spontaneity shown by the other two, if their session looked more like a show, then Riley did not think it was their fault and he did not think it made them any less impressive. They neutralized each other and fought to the end of the round.

The whole time the kid was watching his teammates.

He nodded and when one of them executed a particularly cunning move, he would cry out in admiration and shake his head to himself. Everything seemed to surprise him. The kid was naïve. He lacked cunning. Riley saw that his game, while technically complex, was psychologically simple. Riley wondered how it was going to be. He wondered if he was going to watch him become as deep a fighter as Rivera. He wondered if Rivera was going to try to teach him that too, or if he was going to let him up on pure talent. He shook his head. He tried to remember how young the kid had fought. He tried to remember the feel of his game, the smell of its freshness. Something was telling him it wasn't going to last much longer.

The two older kids were breathing pretty heavy. They walked over and sat down on the benches. They started taking off their gear. Riley's kid sat down next to one of them. He started talking, fast. The older fighter was nodding as he yanked at the Velcro straps on his shinguards. The kid kept talking. He added gestures. The older fighter was done with his gear. He dropped it to one side. He was still nodding and then he stood up and started showing the young kid the set-up to a nice takedown move he had used. The kid watched him. He nodded. He tried it out. He sent the older kid flying to the ground and pinned him. He shouted, grinning.

Murilo turned and looked at them. He called out, gesturing sharply. The two kids scrambled to their feet. Murilo shouted again, voice impatient. The other two fighters stood up a bit slower and then all four of them lined up in the middle of the floor. They sat down, legs spread flat in front of them, and the trainers came and stood behind them. Murilo stood to one side. He watched the kids, frowning. The Q and A started before he had stopped frowning or turned to face the crowd. It pretty much started itself, that's how worked up people were feeling.

"Murilo, can you give us names and ages?"

"Sure." He nodded. He looked at the kids. He pointed. "From the right, that's Roger Lima. He's twenty-five. He's been with us four years now. He fights as a light-heavy. He'll be fighting tomorrow. Next to him, that's Antonio Castillo. Twenty-four. He had some good fights, last year. He's ready, so we'll be stepping things up a bit this year."

The reporters were nodding and scrawling out notes. Murilo glanced at them. He waited for them to catch up. When he was sure they had got it all, he continued. He moved on to the two kids who had fought first.

"Antonio Alves. Another Antonio. Twenty-two. He's very strong, he's one of Rivera's favorite sparring partners. Very good stand-up." His eyes fell on the young kid. "Luis Santos." He paused. He shrugged, a small movement. "Nineteen. We'll debut him tomorrow."

A murmur of excitement spread through the crowd. It whipped through fast, working like nausea. Riley saw Murilo watching them, judging the effect of his words. Riley looked around. He guessed the boys must be pretty glad they stayed. He guessed it had been worth it for them. He ran his hand across his forehead. The temperature felt like it had gone up ten degrees since the Q and A had started. He was sweating, bad.

Murilo cleared his throat. He raised his voice. "The kid's still growing. He's only been training full-time two years."

Another bombshell. Murilo smiled. He shrugged, again. "Before that, we had to let him go to school. We promised his parents."

People laughed, too loud. They grinned at the kid. He stared back at them. He seemed confused.

"Fucking hell," Riley said to Yann.

"He's been sitting on a goldmine."

The crowd was buzzing out on the kid. Riley could feel it. A couple reporters shouted out questions at the same time. Everybody laughed. They tried again.

"Murilo, can you tell us where we'll see these guys fight next? Are they locked into contracts down here?"

"I'm looking at offers now, for all of them. There are no locked contracts. We have been thinking maybe Japan. Rivera always fought in Japan. It has been a very good place for us. But nothing is concluded yet. We'll see. We will look at the offers."

"Is Rivera involved with the day-to-day training at the school?"

"Every day. He is the main force behind the academy. You have to understand, he is like a father to these boys.

They all aspire to be like him one day." He paused. "I'm sorry he's not here today, but he wanted to make a good fight for tomorrow, so he is resting."

"Luis—can you tell us a bit about training at the academy? Do you ever spar with Rivera?"

The kid looked at Murilo. Riley frowned. Murilo leaned over, translating. The kid nodded. He murmured something back, voice straining.

"He says he is very close to Rivera. He is one of his regular sparring partners, so he trains with him almost every day. He trained with him especially hard to prepare for his fight tomorrow."

"And who gets the better of who in practice?" People laughed.

Murilo smiled. "Rivera knocked him out in practice, just the other week." He shrugged. "It was for fun, for a bet."

The kid was staring down at his hands.

"What was the bet?" a reporter shouted out.

Murilo translated the question. The kid said something, again in that soft, high-pitched voice.

"It was over a dog. A puppy?" Murilo shrugged. "I don't know." He said something else to the kid. He turned back to the crowd.

"He bet Rivera a puppy he couldn't knock him out in one round. Rivera, he got the knockout in three minutes. But the kid, he put up a good fight."

"Does he think he'll match Rivera's record one day?"

The kid was shaking his head as Murilo translated. Then he spoke, quickly, voice low. Murilo nodded, patting him on the shoulder.

"He says it is a privilege to train beside him every day. He says it is something he used to dream about, when he was a boy." He paused. He shrugged again. "He says there will never be another fighter like Rivera."

"Murilo—you've got four great young fighters here. That's a hell of a next generation. You got any more you're keeping up your sleeve?"

Murilo smiled. His expression grew expansive. "We have a very big academy down in Brazil. We will open up this academy here, in San Diego. We have the champion in Rivera. We have many other talented fighters. I think we are the strongest team in the world right now. It is a good time for us. In the past couple of years the sport has become big, everywhere in the world. It is getting a lot of attention. We have the fighters to take the sport to the next level." He spoke matter-of-factly.

"Can you tell us a bit about Rivera's condition?"

"He is in great condition. You look at these kids, you think they are impressive—everything they know, Rivera taught them. For the first time in many years, he has no injuries. I am a hundred and fifty percent sure that he will get a quick victory tomorrow. It is a good start for the new gym."

"A hundred and fifty percent?" Yann murmured.

"Yeah." Riley grimaced. "You'd think a hundred would do."

"Any concerns about his opponent?"

"Sure," Murilo said. "Rivera respects his opponent very much. He is a very strong, very tough opponent. Rivera has wanted this rematch for a long time. He wants to prove to everybody that he can defeat him even more decisively than the first time they met." Murilo paused. "This time, it will be a knockout."

Murilo's eyes narrowed. He smiled. "Maybe after he has knocked him out, he will invite him to teach in our new gym. He would be a good addition to the team." He nodded to the kids behind him. "Plus he could help them with their English."

The reporters moved uneasily. Riley snapped his jaw together. Yann nodded.

Josie stepped forward. "Okay, guys, we'll leave a few minutes for photos, and then let's wrap things up—"

The row of tripods inched forward. Slowly, the kids stood up. They looked around, like they weren't quite sure what to do. TFL reps herded them into a row. They stood in formation, hands down, big sweaty grins on their faces. They liked smiling for the cameras; it gave them something to do. The bulbs flashed. The trainers moved them so they'd be standing flush under the Top Team logo. The cameras flashed again. Murilo stood to one side, talking with Josie. Yann nodded to them.

"I'll bet you she's trying to lock down that Luis kid."

"Sure," Riley said. "She can try. But Murilo will contract him in the big leagues."

"Sure he will."

"She'd do well to get any of them locked into a deal."

They walked out the exit. The sun was bright and that was a comfort. They stood by the doors. Yann fumbled in his pocket for a smoke. He nodded to Riley.

"You seen the odds?"

Riley shook his head. "How are they?"

"They're not giving Cal enough credit." He tried to keep his voice light. "I guess you could make a killing if you wanted."

"Well, they're going to be stacked even higher after this." He looked at Yann. His voice was hard. "You know they will. Word spreads fast."

"Sure. I guess it does."

"Every fool in there is going to go out and lay money down on Rivera. I guarantee it."

"Well, it's like I said. You could make a killing if you wanted."

"What about you?"

"You know I'm not a gambling man. Been burned a couple times too many." He said the words lightly. He exhaled, slowly. "You really think Rivera knocked that kid out in practice?"

"I don't know." Riley shook his head. "Kid sure as hell doesn't fight like he's getting knocked out in practice. He fights like he's never been knocked out."

Yann peered into the gym. He shook his head.

"Man. Just look at them. You'd think it was the second coming."

Riley turned his head and looked inside. The reporters had gathered around the Luis kid. He stood almost a head taller than them. He was smiling, he was looking a little more relaxed, but he wasn't enjoying it yet.

"But I'll say. The kid is something special."

Riley nodded. He watched through the glass doors. The kid kept looking at Murilo. Every few seconds he would look at Murilo. Murilo never left his side. He fielded questions. He translated questions. He answered questions for the kid. He laughed and kidded with the reporters and the whole time the kid stood next to him wearing a blank expression on his face. Riley took a good look at him. He was a nice-looking kid. Good looks were rare in the business. The reporters weren't used to it. They kept staring at him. The kid smiled, one last time for the crowd. Then Murilo hustled him off and away from the press. The kid disappeared into the locker room.

Yann nodded to Riley. "Watch out. Here they come."

The doors swung open and people filed out. They were talking, loud, like they couldn't let go of the excitement. Riley smiled grimly. Murilo had put on a good show. He'd got them right where he wanted them. And there was still the weigh-in to come. There was still Rivera.

A couple guys passed. They stopped when they saw Riley and Yann.

"Jesus Christ. Did you see that?"

"The kid is something."

"More than something. I've never seen anything like it."

"No," Riley said. "Me neither."

There was a silence. Awkwardness made it longer. Yann nodded to the two men.

"You guys know anything about this bus?"

"It's leaving as soon as everybody gets packed up."

More people were coming out from the gym. Riley caught snatches of talk. The consensus was solid. The kid could go ahead and start his fan club. He had his charter members, right here. They'd drive his bandwagon to oblivion and back. Riley didn't blame them. Hell, he was pretty inclined to jump on and add to the party. Might as well. He shook his head.

People were passing and they were looking at him. They were smiling and nodding like they felt sorry for him, and Riley hated people feeling sorry for him. Well, of course Rivera's stock was going to go up. He'd trained the kid. For all he knew he'd taught the kid his ground game. For all he knew he'd be whipping out subs come tomorrow. It wasn't impossible. Rivera hadn't had to show the whole of his game. Not for a long time. He was going to show it tomorrow. Riley could already tell.

He turned to Yann abruptly. "I'm going to head off."

"Okay. I'll see you at the weigh-in?"

He nodded. He walked toward his car. He walked so fast he felt like he was running.

7

Riley sat in the car. He watched as people exited the gym. He watched as they climbed onto the bus. They were still talking. Even watching from the car he could tell they were still talking. He sat and he waited until they all got on. The door swung shut. It took just about forever doing it. The bus backed out of the parking lot. He kept watching as it drove off and disappeared down the street.

He exhaled. The air slipped out ragged, catching on the edge of his front teeth. The dentist had done a good job. He'd done a real good job. Riley had used him twice, and then he'd gone on to recommend him to just about every guy he met. He never even remembered about his teeth until times like this. Then all of a sudden he'd hear his breath whistling right up inside his head, like wind flapping through a half-open door.

He sat with his hands on the wheel and he thought about his teeth. The first time he'd almost swallowed them. It had been that fight with Sircello. One of his hard left hooks—it had been all he could do to roll with the punch and spit out his teeth like apple seeds on the way. He'd gone on to win the fight and in the victory pictures he was grinning like some kind of gap-toothed maniac. He'd been too punch-drunk to remember about his teeth. Once it hit him, he shut his mouth and kept it sealed shut, all the way home to the dentist.

The second time he didn't even have to bother spitting them out. The teeth just flew out his mouth and across the ring where they fell to the canvas, pit pat. Between rounds he told his corner to make sure he got his teeth back. His corner kept telling him he had to get his head into the fight. They kept telling him he was going to lose if he didn't hurry up and start making it his fight. He told them to worry about getting his teeth back and leave him to worry about winning the fight. He'd had some kind of stupid idea he could put them back in and save on the dental bill. He thought about it all through the second round and into the third, about how it would work, about how much he would save just not having to make the crowns, wondering if maybe the dentist would give him some kind of a discount seeing as how he was shaping up to be a repeat customer. He figured it was the thinking that cost him the fight. The thinking and the worrying about his teeth.

Well, it could have been worse. It could have been like Atkinson. Snorting teeth through the nose while the television producers shouted for a cut. It could have been a hell of a lot worse. He had to remember that. He could have shat them out of his ass, for all he knew.

He switched the ignition on and sat, hands on the wheel.

Oh boy, he thought. Oh *boy*.

He could almost pretend it hadn't happened. He could almost do it. After all, it amounted to nothing. There was no real information. There was nothing concrete. He hadn't even seen Rivera. He thought about this. He had seen—what had he seen? He'd seen some kids. Some good, talented kids. The only thing he'd seen was proof that Rivera was developing considerably as a trainer. And even then he didn't *know*.

He leaned back his head and closed his eyes. He thought about the young kid. Luis Santos. Murilo had trained some of the biggest names in the sport and there was a rancor in that, but this kid counted beyond. He was past the tally. The kid had the magic. He could feel it now, all up inside him. He *saw* the kid, up inside his head, punching, kicking, moving like he was playing over and over on repeat, and the feeling swelled up in him again. Maybe it was something you never got over. Maybe it stayed with you forever, just like true love. He grimaced. That was his caustic side getting the better of him. *Every day is a holiday because you're married to me!* The old jingle popped into his head and it stayed there, minus the acid. The acid just floated off.

Well, it was something. Seeing what the next generation was going to look like. He thought about it and then he realized how old he was. How old Cal was. The numbers just hit him in the face. It was like the game had moved past both of them.

He opened his eyes and waited for a moment and then he backed the car out and drove. He knew now what he had always known. Cal could not win against Rivera. It was impossible. There wasn't going to be any getting back on track. He'd made a mistake.

Riley would believe when no one else would believe. He wasn't like some guys. He had no problem with believing. He'd believe in his fighters so that they didn't have to believe in themselves. He'd do it for them. He loved it, the believing. It was everything to him. But this time he was beat.

He drove. He was tired. He was very, very tired.

Fighting wasn't down to chance. It wasn't even down to heart. It was down to skill, size, conditioning, preparation. Mental state. Nine times out of ten Riley knew the outcome of a fight before it happened. Everything was there to know. A fight was just a series of logical conclusions. You couldn't afford to believe in miracles. Miracles were a dead end. You knew what was coming. Going into a fight, you just always knew what was coming.

It was the oldest trap in the game and he'd walked right into it. He'd been fooled by the story of the way things used to be. He'd been waiting for the second act in Cal's career. The second act that would be just like the first act and mean they could keep on going like nothing was ever gonna change. Well, it was too late. It wasn't going to happen. The chance had come and gone while he'd been telling himself goddamned stories.

He sat back and he looked at the numbers again. He realized that Cal was old. He was twenty-nine. He realized that he was older than Rivera, by a couple years. It took him by surprise. For some reason he'd kept on seeing him like he was young.

He wasn't young. He thought about the fight and he thought the kid would probably get knocked out. Cal had never been knocked out but he had a feeling this time it was gonna happen. He thought about Rivera knocking out Murilo's kid in under three minutes and he shook his head. He used to believe Cal couldn't get knocked out. Just like he used to believe Cal couldn't get beat. Well, he figured tomorrow he would see him get knocked out for the first time in his life. He thought about Cal and he thought about his age and then he knew his body wouldn't stand for it. All of a sudden he saw that it wouldn't make it through.

The whole thing was a mistake. A big fucking mistake. His palms slid down the wheel and his mouth went dry. He'd thought he was doing the right thing. He'd really believed it was for the best. He should have known better. He should have seen the situation for what it really was and he should have let him go. Letting go was the harder thing. He should have faced up to the harder thing, a long time ago.

He closed his eyes. The story of a comeback, the story of the rematch—he'd just used that to keep them together. They'd been together for practically as long as he could remember. It was everything he knew. There was never going to be a good place for it to end. He was never going to be ready. But there was only so much time you could buy. It was ending now, and he couldn't stop it.

Riley breathed through his teeth, again. He stared at the road. He thought about Cal, waiting at the motel in Tijuana. Waiting to hear about Rivera. He had no idea what he was going to say to him. He figured the kid would know the most of it just from looking at him. But what was he going to *say* to him? He couldn't see the words. They didn't come to him.

Fuck it. For a long moment the feeling took hold of him and it was the most obvious thing in the world. Fuck it, turn the car around and *go*. It was like the road was made for it. The freeway was wide and open and he was driving fast and there was nothing to see for miles. Maybe Tijuana was only fifteen minutes away but it seemed a lot farther from where he was now. That was what the border did. Once he crossed the border it would be too late, but if he turned around now, he could just drive back north like none of this had ever happened—

He accelerated the car without knowing it. He shifted over a lane.

Sometimes it was like sticking it out was a thing you did because you didn't know what else to do. They didn't have to be here. There was no reason. They were here because he'd made a mistake. That was the only reason. He thought about it and then he knew that Cal had never wanted the fight. Not in the way he'd wanted it. He had led Cal into it. The kid had only followed. He'd gone along with it, and nothing more.

There was a low wailing and then he caught a flash of light in the rearview mirror.

Just his fucking luck. He eased his foot onto the brake. Not too sudden, not too guilty seeming, but it was already too late. The cop was pulling in right behind him and he knew it wasn't going to do him any good, the ten or twenty miles he had shaved off the speedometer. He slowed to a stop on the shoulder and then switched the ignition off. His eye slid to the clock. Way past twelve. The day was just eating up the time. It would be one before he made it back to Tijuana.

The cop rapped on the car window. Riley looked at him. Big guy, with a gray mustache and shades. Older than him. That was a surprise. He was just getting used to all the cops looking like they were young enough to be his kids, but this guy was old enough to be his father. Riley rolled the window down.

"Driver's license," the cop said. His voice was gruff, and he was wheezing in the lungs as he spoke. He spoke like speaking was an exertion and he was leaning hard into Riley's car like standing was too.

Riley nodded. He reached for his wallet and passed his

license to the cop. The cop took it and walked back to his patrol car. Riley sat in the car. He was too old to give any lip and he was too ugly to talk his way out of it. Sometimes the younger guys, the kids, they'd let him go. He'd go paternal on them and then they'd let him go. He had a feeling that wasn't going to work on this cop. He had a feeling this cop wasn't going to be shy like that. He was just going to have to swallow the fine. Claim it as expenses. The thought made him laugh.

The cop was back. He kept his shades on. It made Riley nervous. The cop being able to see right into his eyes, and him not being able to see anything back. The cop parked a hand on the roof of the car and leaned into the window again. Riley didn't like people touching his car, but then he wasn't in a position to argue, and he had a feeling the cop knew that. He looked up at him.

"You have any idea how fast you were going?"

Riley nodded.

"Where you headed?"

"Tijuana."

"What business you got in Tijuana?"

"I got to corner a guy in a fight."

"A fight, huh?"

"Yeah. I'm running late for the weigh-ins, that's why I was kind of driving in a hurry."

He looked up. The cop was staring down at him from behind his shades.

"Not that I'm trying to make excuses," he added.

"You get yourself a visa for that?"

"Excuse me?"

"I said, you get yourself a visa to work in Mexico?"

Riley paused. He sat back into the seat. "Officer, I'm not getting paid to do this. I'm not working. I'm just doing a friend a favor."

The cop nodded. "Okay," he said. "Sure you are." He paused. "You stay there." Riley nodded.

The cop turned and walked back to his car. He sat inside for a while, taking notes or something. Keeping himself busy looking official. Riley fidgeted. He watched him in the rearview mirror. The cop looked up and saw him. Riley looked away.

He heard a car door slam. The cop was walking back toward him. He leaned up against the door again. That made the third time. Maybe he couldn't do anything about it, but that didn't mean he wasn't going to keep count. The cop took off his sunglasses. He settled in good. Riley didn't move. He didn't look at his face. He didn't look into his eyes. He stared straight ahead and waited for him to speak.

The cop squinted. "You know, I used to go in for a bit of boxing myself."

"Yeah?" Riley kept his voice even.

"Yeah. Hell, it was years ago, when I was young and fit, before I packed on all this weight. Used to train up at a gym in San Jose, back in the day." He nodded to Riley. "You a trainer or what?"

"Yeah, I train guys."

"You got a gym?"

"I got a gym."

"Your guy got a good chance of winning tonight?"

"Sure he's got a good chance."

"He a winner?"

"Sure he's a winner."

The cop nodded and leaned back away from the car. He looked at Riley. "Well," he said. Then he stopped. Riley bit back a wince. He hated this shit.

"Maybe I'll look up your place some time." The cop placed his hand over the edge of the door. He had the license hanging down between his fingers.

"Sure," Riley said. "I'll keep an eye out for you."

"Good luck with your fight."

"Thanks."

The cop handed Riley his license and walked back to his car. Riley watched in the rearview mirror as he got in and slipped his shades back on. He waited until the cop had driven out before starting the car. He slipped into the freeway and made it into Tijuana fifteen minutes later.

Swinging into the parking lot of the motel, he clocked the time again. Clearing his throat, he swung the car door open and walked to their room, striding hard. He jumped the stairs two at a time and didn't slow his pace all the way to their room. He rapped on the door once before pushing it open.

Cal was lying on the bed. He was playing a puzzle. One

of those metal knot ones, Cal was crazy for them. He played them all the time. He didn't look up when Riley walked in. He flicked one piece over and around and then through another. He pulled the other piece round and then back under. The whole of the mess unfolded into a circular link. He looked at it. He looked pleased. Riley cleared his throat and slammed the door shut.

Cal looked at Riley. "So," he said. "That bad?"

Riley shrugged. He tossed his keys onto the bed. "Rivera didn't show up."

"He didn't show up?" Cal frowned. He looked back down at the puzzle. He moved the pieces until the whole thing was one knotted mass. Then he placed it carefully on the bedside table. He folded his hands together and looked up at Riley.

"Yeah." Riley cleared his throat. "It was a no-show."

"So why were you gone so long?"

Riley paused. "I got talking to some of the guys. Ran into Yann." He tried to speak casual. "Decided I might as well stay and watch Rivera's training partners. They turned up in his place."

He looked at Cal. The kid was sitting up now and watching him. He waited for him to continue.

"They looked good."

"I bet," Cal said.

"They looked real good," he repeated.

Cal nodded. He kept looking at Riley.

"What else?"

"Nothing much. Got stopped on the way back by some cop. That slowed me down a bit."

"Well, there's still a lot of time till the weigh-in."

Riley looked at Cal. He could hear the tension in his voice. He sat down on the bed next to him.

"Something bothering you?"

Cal shrugged. He shook his head.

"I saw the odds."

Riley was surprised. "You looked up the odds?"

"Yeah."

"Where?"

Cal shrugged. "They're pretty funny."

"Yeah, well, the bookies are out there to make money, not to call fights."

"Isn't it the same thing?" He didn't wait for an answer. He moved his head. "I know I'm the underdog. But they're overdoing it, you know."

Riley passed a hand over his face. He felt the tiredness sink into him again. He looked at Cal.

"It's nothing to worry about."

"I know."

"I mean, it's not something to get hung up about."

"I know."

He stayed sitting next to Cal. Cal picked up the puzzle again and started unlocking it. He moved his head back and forth, rolling it through the neck. Then his mind settled into the puzzle and his eyes cleared up. Riley watched him. He looked so young. He wasn't young. But he looked it, just now. He was frowning a little as he tried to remember how the puzzle worked. Riley hesitated.

Cal looked up.

"What is it?"

His eyes were perfectly clear. Riley looked at him. He tried to think of the words. His mouth was dry and he swallowed. Then he shook his head and stood up.

"Come on. Let's get going. The afternoon's going to be a long one."

8

They held the weigh-ins in a building around the corner from the Caliente. Cal stood by himself. Riley was a couple feet away, talking. Cal could hear his voice. He didn't listen but he could hear his voice distinctly.

Rivera was standing on the other side of the room. He was surrounded by his team. It was impossible to know how long he had been there. He'd been there when they arrived. He stood as if he'd been there forever. His arms were hanging down and he had his back very straight and his head thrust forward. He was just standing. He didn't seem to move at all.

Cal watched him. He looked much as he expected. Very little about Rivera had changed over the years. His face and body had remained the same. He had the same pale eyes and fight-flattened nose. His arms and legs hung off his body like wiring and that was also the same. He looked at Rivera and he thought he looked in good condition. He thought he looked ready.

One of his trainers was talking to him. Rivera watched him as he spoke. Then he raised his head and looked around the room. Only a second—Cal could count it. He bent his head back down. The trainer was still talking. Rivera nodded, once. The movement didn't travel above or beneath the neck. His face hardly changed.

Riley came up to him.

"You doing okay?"

He nodded.

Riley glanced in Rivera's direction.

"Looks like he's dropped a few pounds."

Cal nodded again. Riley cleared his throat.

"I guess we'll see if it makes a difference."

Somebody from the promotion told them to sit down. He led Cal to his seat, as Riley branched off into another row a couple feet back. Cal sat down. He looked around him. There were a lot of fighters. He watched them. He watched them talking to their trainers. He looked at the stage set up front. There were chairs and microphones and microphone stands. There was a banner with the promotion logo printed in red and black. It was big. It practically covered the whole stage.

The staff were moving to get the last fighters to their seats. Some guy was explaining to them how the weigh-ins would work. "Same as always, guys. When your name is called, step on up. There's a screen that you can strip down behind. Get weighed in, pose for the cameras, step back down. Pretty straightforward." Nobody was listening to him. The fighters were busy talking. They all seemed to know each other. The guy continued. "So everybody's clear. That's great. Okay. That's great." He stopped. He looked at the fighters. None of them looked back. He turned and headed off abruptly.

Cal watched the guy walk off. He felt sorry for him. You could tell fighters what to do and they would do it. They would even be friendly while they were doing it. But it was a tough crowd. They were just waiting for you to leave.

Cal waited for things to get going. He was used to the weigh-ins. He was used to the press conferences. It was familiar ground and he knew his way through it. He sat back into his chair. There was always a distracted feeling to the weigh-ins, like nobody sitting there could pay enough attention to make sense of the proceedings. The fighters sat through the sessions, doing as they were told and waiting for them to end.

Some guy up front was talking. He was talking a long time. The fighters were getting restless. Conversation was starting up between them again. They were polite. They kept their voices low. On the whole fighters were a pretty polite bunch.

The guy was still talking. Conversation got louder. It got real. Now it was sentences rather than snatches. There were guys practically delivering monologues. Some fighters were like that. They liked telling stories. They liked their words. You couldn't shut them up once they got started. They just kept running over their words.

Cal kept his eyes low. He didn't want to talk. They had divided the fighters into two groups set on either side of the room. They were split up by matches. Red corner versus blue corner. He was in the blue corner. Rivera was in the red corner. Rivera would be sitting on the other side of the room. He would be close. It would be a matter of yards.

He hesitated. Through the hesitation he could feel the guy sitting next to him. He could feel him wanting to talk. It had come up from nowhere. He hadn't even noticed the guy before.

"It's funny."

The guy sitting next to him was looking at him hard, leaning forward so that he could look right into his face.

"Man. It's funny."

Cal looked up. The guy was shaking his head. He shook it in the same way he had looked at Cal. Like he couldn't stop, once he had started. The face itself was solid. Nothing in it moved. It looked just about the way Cal expected. Everything had been broken and then put back together. Everything still worked, it was just that the face had got lost in the middle of it all. Fighters started to look like that, after a while. Like their faces were trying to remember the way they used to look. The guy was young but he didn't look young in the face. No fighter looked young in the face, after a while.

"I watched you, all the time. I seen you on television so many times it's like I know you. Watched all your fights. Couldn't wait for you to fight."

Cal nodded. He cleared his throat.

"It's just that it's funny, you know. Funny seeing you now, in real life. You look totally the same. But you look kind of different too."

"I guess it does that." Cal paused. He looked at the guy. He added, "Television."

"Couldn't stop looking at you. It's weird, you know? Like you look the same. Like I knew it was you right away. But you look different too." The guy shook his head. "Crazy to think I'm fighting on the same card as you, man! Shit, this is a big day for me." He grinned. The mouth moved, but everything else stayed the same. The eyes stayed the same. Cal nodded.

"Who you fighting?"

"Lima. One of the Top Team guys."

"Never seen him."

"He's tough."

"Sure. They all are."

"It'll be a tough fight for me. But I'm ready. You know?"

"Sure." Cal nodded. He looked down, like it would end the conversation.

The guy didn't want the conversation to end. Now the actual weigh-ins themselves were starting. The fighters were going up, two by two, one from each side of the room, starting with the undercard. He and Rivera would be last. There was a ways to go yet. There were ten matches on the card.

"You cutting weight?"

Cal looked up.

"What?"

"You cutting weight?"

"Nah." He paused. "We're fighting at 205."

"Rivera cutting weight?"

"Think so."

There was a pause. Cal cleared his throat.

"Man. I'm cutting fifteen pounds for this fight."

Cal nodded.

"I'm not some wrestler. I don't know shit about cutting weight. I'm feeling all funny."

"Just drink lots of water once the weigh-ins are over. And try not to piss it all out."

"Yeah. I heard that."

The guy was nodding. He was silent, like he was too busy nodding to be talking. Like he couldn't be doing both at once. They watched as the fighters stepped onto the scale. They watched as they bundled up their fists for the camera. Cal couldn't hear the doctor as he announced the weights. The sound of his announcement was swallowed by a polite smattering of applause. The whole thing stopped making sense, when you looked at it like this.

He jerked his chin at Cal. "You ever not make weight?"

"No."

"Yeah, I guess you wouldn't have that problem." The guy's eyes were vacant.

Cal paused. He looked at the guy. He looked at his

eyes. He said, "Don't worry." The words didn't seem enough. He added, "Anyway, if you don't make weight, they'll give you a couple hours."

The guy shook his head. "Man, I can't lose any more. I'm starving! I want to eat. I'm feeling all funny," he repeated.

Cal shrugged. Nobody liked cutting weight. Nobody did it for fun.

They were on his row now. Two fighters had stood and gone up. Two fighters were circling back after weighing in. They dropped down into their seats. There was a subtle release in the movement. Everybody was making weight. It was going okay. It shook guys up when a fighter didn't make weight. Nobody liked it. It felt like a bad omen, for everybody involved.

They were coming up on Cal. The guy next to him stood up. Cal nodded to him and he nodded back. He was nervous. Cal was glad he was leaving. He couldn't stand watching the nervousness cave the guy's head in. He sat and he waited for them to call his name. He didn't think about Rivera. He cleared his head. He sat and he waited.

A murmur ran through the room. He looked up. The guy who had been sitting next to him was stepping off the scales. He was standing in his trunks. The official ringside doctor was readjusting the weights. A young fighter was standing at the far side of the stage. He was smiling at someone in the crowd. That had to be Lima. There was no malice in the smile but he saw the guy watching him. He saw him catching the smile.

The guy passed a hand across his mouth. The doctor gestured for him to step back onto the scales. He did it quickly, stepping hard like he wanted to get it over with. The weights on the scale bounced. The doctor raised a hand to adjust them. He flicked them over. First the hundred-pound measure. Then the tens and the fives and then he was just sliding them back and forth like he was looking for a way for the guy to make weight. He looked for it all down the length of the scale and then he stopped and shook his head.

The guy stepped off the scales. He turned around. He looked like he wasn't sure where to go. The reporters were scrawling down notes. The doctor announced the weight. Three pounds over. Cal shook his head. It wouldn't be easy to cut that kind of weight. He figured they'd give him a couple of hours. Even if he did make weight he'd be too exhausted from the cutting to put on a good fight.

The guy was ushered off the stage. He was hustled out of the room by his trainers. Cal figured they'd be taking him straight down to the sauna. It depended on how much water weight he had left to lose. He turned his head to watch as he walked out. All the fighters did. It was embarrassing. He felt for the guy. He seemed like the kind of guy who would feel the embarrassment. He had barely turned back around when they called his name.

He stood up. On the other side of the room he saw Rivera stand up. They stood for only a second—it was funny, the effect of hearing his name called out in an unfa-

miliar voice, over the scuffle and boom of the microphone—but it seemed to take more than that. The cameras started flashing immediately. That held them there—
they were making pictures without meaning to. They
moved forward, at the same time.

He watched from the corner pocket of his vision as
Rivera disappeared behind the screen. He moved abruptly,
like he was tired of their being synched up. It wasn't
planned. It was just coincidence. The last thing Cal saw was
his back, disappearing behind the screen.

Cal stepped behind the screen. It only took him a
moment to strip off his clothes. Even so, when he stepped
out Rivera was there already, chest and feet bare, muscles
tense, weight shifting from foot to foot. It was like there
was something snapping through him, vertically. Cal
could almost see it. He could almost *hear* it standing
across the stage from him.

When Rivera was still he was so still that you could not
imagine him moving. When he was moving, like this, you
could not imagine him still. Cal remembered this. Then
he looked away. He would weigh in first. Rivera was
standing by the scales. He would have to pass Rivera to do
it. He started walking up. He walked up too early, before
they were ready for him.

He passed Rivera. Normally fighters would look at the
body. They would get a measure of shape and size, of
conditioning and muscle mass—they would try to pick up
the kind of concrete information that could be strategi-

cally used in the fight. Rivera didn't look past the eyes. He didn't look any farther. He only looked at the eyes and his gaze didn't flicker.

Cal weighed in at 198.

He stepped off the scales. He turned to the cameras. They told him to wait—they would need to get pictures of him and Rivera together. He waited. He watched Rivera move forward to get weighed.

He expected him to weigh in at exactly 205. He would weigh in at 205 and he would hit 220 for the fight. There would be a difference of twenty-two pounds. Rivera would make him feel it like fifty. Cal was expecting this. On any other fighter Cal could negotiate twenty-two pounds. He had done it, the whole of his career—but with Rivera, it was more than just a weight difference. It was opening things up. There was no way of knowing how it would play. There was no way of knowing how Rivera would use his advantage.

Rivera stepped up. He stepped up delicately, almost mincingly—he always weighed in that way. That was the vanity. He couldn't afford the vanity in the ring, but it came out in other places. Rivera saw himself. The thought struck Cal—Rivera saw himself, all the time. Cal never saw himself. But Rivera, he saw himself, as a physical object being observed. That was why the vanity came out at the weigh-in.

He weighed in bang on 205.

He stepped down and turned to the cameras. Rivera

stood with his arms down and his hands loose—Rivera never mugged for the camera. He never flexed his muscles. The muscles were standing out anyway.

The cameras were going crazy. Cal looked at him. For the first time he really looked at him. He looked incredible. He couldn't believe how strong he looked. Rivera had a fighter's physique, he always had, but lately he'd been turning up at fights looking heavy, carrying a few extra pounds. Riley was right. He'd lost those pounds. It had made his body snap together. It had made everything cohere. He had not looked so good for a long time. Not since the beginning of his career, when he defeated Cal, and the year or two after.

They brought Cal forward. He moved until he stood a foot away from Rivera and then he stopped. They turned to face each other. They stood face-to-face. They looked each other in the eye.

The fear scrabbled into him hard. He thought to himself that he was not afraid of Rivera. He thought to himself that he was only afraid of the moment. He was not afraid of Rivera. But even as he was not afraid he was taking in his size—he was thinking how long it had been since he'd fought an opponent so large, he was thinking that he had not, in the four years since, fought anyone close to Rivera's level, and even so he had taken many losses—and he was taking in his power and his strength and the fear was now concentrating around Rivera himself.

The cameras kept flashing. He blinked through the

flashing. He might be facing the beating of a lifetime tomorrow. The thought was like a blow to the head. He looked at Rivera and all he saw was violence. He gave off violence. It was everything about him. The capacity for violence—that was all there was. He thought about stepping into the ring with him tomorrow and it seemed an unthinkable thing. They'd made a mistake. He looked at Rivera and he knew they'd made a mistake.

The fear rushed in again. He thought probably Rivera could see it. He thought probably everybody in the room could see it. The nightmares were of his own dreaming but the fear was more than that. The fear went further. It was in his body, like it had set into his blood. It was in the room, in the crowd, it was thick in the air he was breathing. He was shaking as he breathed and he closed his eyes.

They stepped down from the stage and returned to their seats. He sat down, body leaden. He couldn't think. Some guy stepped up and thanked the crowd. He listened to him but he couldn't take any of it in. Then the staff were everywhere and the fighters were being moved past the press so they couldn't be stopped. They were taken out separately and escorted all the way until they cleared the room. As he walked he saw Riley fall in line behind him.

Riley looked at him. The kid looked like he'd been run over by a truck. His eyes were blank and his face was soft and still. He stood there and it barely moved. Riley's stomach turned just looking at him. He cleared his throat.

"Well, that was something."

Cal nodded. He wet his lips.

"It's over."

They walked outside. Riley's head was going numb. The kid had looked shit scared up there. He'd stood on the stage and he'd looked out into the crowd like he was looking for someone to give him a reason not to do it. Like he was looking for someone to step in and stop him.

Cal breathed out hard. Riley swallowed.

"You okay?"

"I'm fine."

"It's getting pretty hot."

"He looked good."

Riley was silent.

"I thought he looked real good. Didn't you?"

"I thought he looked good."

Cal nodded. Then he turned and looked at Riley. He stopped. They both stopped. Riley breathed out slow. He thought Cal had to know. He looked into his face. He looked for the signs. He tried to see what he was thinking. He thought he knew Cal pretty good. He thought he knew how to read him. But right now all he could see was the fear. It was clouding over everything.

"The fight's tomorrow."

Riley nodded. He was silent

"It doesn't feel like it. It doesn't feel like it's tomorrow."

He nodded again. He didn't look at Cal. Cal turned abruptly and started walking. Riley stood for a moment. Then he turned and followed him. It was hot. November in Tijuana—he'd have thought it would be cooler. Cal was walking fast in front of him. He let him walk. He let the kid walk and he followed him, slowly from behind.

9

It was November and the sun rose at six. Five minutes to six and it was dark. Six and the outline of the street was visible. Another five minutes and things were standing out on their own. Buildings. Billboards. Trees. Ten minutes and you could see Tijuana again. It was a different Tijuana to the Tijuana you saw during the day and the Tijuana you saw at night, but it was still Tijuana.

Cal stood and looked at the light coming down on the motel. He stood and looked at it coming down the roof. Then he turned and began walking down the street. The sidewalk was just a couple feet wide and the street was a big one but now the traffic was dead and the road empty and he walked without worrying about the cars. He walked west. He walked in the opposite direction of the warehouse. The opposite direction of the Caliente. He just wanted to walk and watch the light.

The heat was low. The heat would pick up in the day and then it would die back down and by the time the fight was on it would be cool again. Ten minutes had passed and now there was enough light to read signs by. There was no color in the light. It was just a layer of gray. Early-morning light. It took the edge off things. It made everything look a little blurry. Cal blinked his eyes to see right. It took a lot of blinking and by the time his eyes had adjusted the light had moved on.

He walked. It was the morning of the fight and his stomach was hard and empty like he hadn't eaten in days. His head was light and his throat was dry and he had to keep swallowing to breathe. He concentrated on walking and he watched the light. It was running up against everything. It was getting stuck on the high-rises and the two-story billboards. He could feel the heat of the day, picking up already. It was going to be a hot one.

He saw a couple posters for the fight. They looked new and wet, like they had just been put up. They were catching the light and he could see the pictures and read the letters clearly. They had pasted strips of paper across the posters with the word VENDIO written in red letters. He walked a bit more and he saw a billboard advertising the fights and he saw a few more posters and then he saw a whole wall of them, dampened by the rain and faded by the sun and crumpled up in parts.

He stopped and looked at the posters and then he almost threw up. It just came up in him. The feeling. Like his insides had contracted very fast and without warning. He clamped his throat closed and swallowed. The feeling kept jolting up and he kept swallowing and swallowing until the feeling went away and all that was left was the taste of bile in his mouth. It set his head spinning but the feeling wasn't unfamiliar. It wasn't unknown. He made himself look at the posters again. He stood there like he was never going to move. Then he turned and walked again.

The streets were still quiet but it was a little like the city was waking up. He started seeing people. Just here and there. He saw an old guy waiting for the bus. There were no buses in sight but he was waiting. A couple blocks later he saw a woman walking down the street. She walked fast and then she disappeared around the corner just as fast. The sun was higher. It was looking more like morning now.

He came across a bunch of old women cleaning the sidewalks. They were throwing pails of water onto the ground and then they were sweeping the water up with old wooden brooms. They moved out of the way as he walked by. He nodded hello. They nodded back. He stepped through the water. When he had passed they continued sweeping. He could hear the swishing of the brooms and the splash of water.

He kept walking. He didn't know where he was going but he kept on. He walked until the buildings fell back and it was mostly empty lots full of trash and broken rubble. He walked up toward the hills. He walked like he was going to keep walking forever. There was no end to the landscape and if he wanted he could just keep going. The thought occurred to him. There was nothing to stop him. It could be the rest of his life. He could just keep walking and never turn back.

He stopped. He stared out at the land. He thought about walking and he thought about Rivera and then Rivera was all he could see. He filled his mind. He just snapped into the frame and he filled it. A spasm ran down his neck and he closed his eyes. He tried to imagine the fight and all that came to him was a blurred darkness and Rivera in the middle of it. That was all he got. He felt his pulse, low in his belly like his heart had dropped right down. He opened his eyes again. He concentrated on his breathing.

He looked out at the city. He stood there and he thought maybe he would run. He thought about what he would be putting his body through in the fight. He had spent the whole of his life conditioning his body to receive punishment. Now he was older and he knew the punishment wasn't enough. It used to be he almost looked forward to it. Now he looked at the pain and he didn't know what it was for. He didn't know what it did and he thought probably it didn't do anything at all.

The taste of bile was still in his mouth and he swallowed to get rid of it. The fear was strong and he felt it like a tightness in the throat. His eyes were watering. He looked at the city through the wetness in his eyes. He kept looking and then he knew he wasn't going to run. He knew it wasn't possible. He was sick with fear. He had no more love for the game. He had no more heart and he had no more hunger. But he was conditioned to the fight. The habit was strong.

He thought about the life he had led, and all those years of training. He thought he'd been training his body and his mind but really he'd been training the habit. Habit was the strongest thing inside him right now. It was overriding the fear. It was overriding the logic and the want and it was overriding the need. There was nothing he could do about it. He knew he would see it through. It was the only thing he knew how to do.

He looked into the light, and he breathed out slow. He thought about when he was a boy. He used to watch the fights on television. They played the last Sunday of every month. He remembered looking forward to them. He watched them with his brothers. His mother made chili dip and chicken wings and they piled into the den to watch. They each had their favorite fighters. They cheered them on. It was like they knew them. It was like they were more real to them than anything else.

When the fights were over they would go outside to play. Their house was on a big wide road and there were never any cars. They would scuffle around in the dirt playing champion. They would step into the chalk-drawn ring. Whoever was playing champion would swing and then the other boy would collapse to the ground. They loved playing champion. They would raise their fists into the air the way they did on television. They would circle and feint and then they would raise their fists again.

When he thought about his childhood, that was what came to him. He remembered the smell of food from the kitchen. He remembered the sound of his uncle working in the garage while the fights played. He sat in front of the television. He pressed his face close. Close, like he could never get close enough. He stared into the screen. It was like everything he wanted was inside. It was like if he could just find a way to push through, he'd be perfectly happy.

His eyes were still watering and now he blinked to clear away the wetness. He blinked until his eyes were half dry and he could see the light on the city, clear and hard and bright. He had walked a long way. The city was spread out before him. He tried to see the Caliente from where he was but he had walked too far and it was lost in the buildup of houses and high-rises. He kept looking for it anyway. He stood and he looked. The light was spilling everywhere. There were no shadows to the place. There was something strange about the way the landscape looked but he wasn't sure what it was.

All he saw was the light. He looked up into the cloud-less sky. There was no sun, anywhere. Tijuana was like that. The closest he would come to seeing the sun was now, in the morning. That was the closest he would ever come. Cal stood there for a little while longer. He believed he was brave. He still thought he could be. He looked for the sun. Then he turned and started walking back.

•   •   •

Riley woke up at seven. It had been that way for a few years now. No matter what, he woke at seven. It was like having an alarm clock nailed inside his head. Seven rang, and he was up.

There was light everywhere. It was already hot. As he sat up the covers slipped down to his waist. He sat, skin bare to the light. He could feel the heat gathering on his skin. He could feel every inch, as it traveled down the length of his arms and over to his belly. He sat and enjoyed the feeling. The feeling of the sun on his skin—it was an old feeling, from a long time ago. It took him somewhere. He couldn't say where, but it took him somewhere, way back.

The room was very quiet. There was nothing inside the room except the feeling of the sun and the feeling of his skin. His mind wandered over the emptiness. It didn't mean anything, and he liked that. He didn't get to feel the emptiness that often anymore. He remembered that the windows were open, and he thought that must be the reason for the heat feeling the way it did. Heat always felt different coming through plain. A glass window did more than you thought.

He stared out the window. He was in no hurry to get out of bed. He didn't need to hurry. It gave you all kinds of extra hours, getting up early. That was the thing. He used to hate the extra hours. Then he got used to it. He found ways to fill the hours. They said it was part of getting older. He guessed they meant the time, or maybe they meant the ways you found to fill it. He figured once you got used to the extra time, you were pretty much sunk. You got old having extra time. Having extra time, and getting used to it.

He pushed the covers back and got out of bed. He looked around the room. The other bed was empty. Cal was gone.

He sat back down. Anyway all he could hear was the quiet buzzing around inside his head. Dead quiet. That's what it was. Couldn't see it any other way, now. Couldn't see it like empty, couldn't see it with the light, couldn't see it in the way of a few minutes ago. A few minutes ago was gone, like it never even bothered existing.

He tried to think what it meant, Cal being gone so early. He tried to think what it would mean for the fight. He didn't want to think about it but he did. He couldn't help it. The fight came back and it changed everything. He couldn't stop the thinking. He felt himself waking up, for real this time.

He checked the time—7:03. He couldn't think where the kid could be, this hour in the morning. It was early. Too early. It was the morning of the fight. He wouldn't have gone out for a run. He looked at the clock again.

He must have gone out to get some air. The room was close. It made sense. It was natural. Probably he was standing right outside the room. Standing on the balcony and enjoying the morning air. Shaking out the sleep. Riley stood up and went to the door. It was only five or six steps.

He swung the door open and looked outside. There was nobody there. He looked both ways. He stepped out onto the balcony and looked down, into the parking lot, and then he looked both ways again before stepping back into the room.

He shut the door. He sat back down on the bed. He checked the time. Hardly a minute had passed. Less than a minute. He watched the time click from 7:03 to 7:04.

He closed his eyes and rubbed at them. He didn't open them. He didn't think he could stand to see more time passing. The kid had to have been gone a while. Riley slept light toward morning, he always did. If he'd left any time recent, he would have heard him. He would have woken up.

He looked at the clock again. He couldn't stop himself. He sighed. The sigh came out like a groan. It came with all kinds of noises. The noises didn't used to be there. He realized that, halfway through. He felt old. He felt like an old man, sitting there on the bed, bare-chested in his boxer shorts and waiting. He was an old man. He could see his age, everywhere around him. In the sheets and the comforter and the carpet under his feet.

He passed a hand across his face. He stared out the window. He thought about the fight. He thought there were still ways of it not happening. They were ugly ways but they were ways. Maybe it would end the kid's career but he guessed the kid's career was ending either way. He didn't believe the fight could save the kid. Not anymore.

Riley sat on the bed. He thought about more than the fight. He looked at the light coming in through the window and he couldn't keep the thinking away. His jaw was trembling and he bit down hard to stop it. A trainer was supposed to protect his fighter. He was supposed to make sure his fighter didn't get any more hurt than he had to. That was the promise. That was what kept a fighter and a trainer together.

He heard the sound of the key in the lock and he stood up abruptly. His knees shot up and left him there. Just standing. He was just standing there, in the middle of the room, when Cal walked in.

The sight of the kid coming through doorway just about burst into his head. The relief of it did. He felt like running up and hugging the kid. Running up and shaking him and hugging him and asking him where he'd gone and why he'd done it, disappearing like that.

He sat back down, abruptly. Cal looked at him. Only for a second. Then he kicked the door shut and tossed the key onto the bedside table.

"You go out?"

The question slipped out of him. He couldn't keep it back. He heard his voice, outside of him. He heard it asking the question. The voice was high and nervous and it came out sounding like a whine. He was turning into someone else before his own eyes. He grimaced and turned away.

"Just for a walk."

Cal's voice was low and scratchy, like it was the first thing he'd said all morning. The scratchiness was okay. The scratchiness was good. It meant he hadn't been up too long. It meant his sleep wasn't that far off. Riley swallowed.

"How'd you sleep?"

"Good."

"What time did you get up?"

"Six-thirty."

Cal paused. Then he smiled at Riley. He shook his head.

"Your snoring."

"What?"

"Your snoring." He shook his head again. "You should think about seeing a doctor for that. It's worse than I remember. Could be something that needs looking at."

"Fuck off."

But he was grinning at the kid and the kid was smiling back at him. He looked at the clock—7:10. It was only ten minutes. Ten minutes was long enough to take you through your paces. He looked back up at the kid.

"Well."

"Yeah."

"It's early."

"Guess so."

Cal lay down on the bed. He pulled the pillows out and piled them under his head. He did it slow. Like they had been out of place, and he was putting them back. He laid his head down. He closed his eyes.

"Let's watch some television."

He said it with his eyes closed. Riley looked at him.

"Okay."

He looked at him again. His eyes were still closed. Riley reached for the remote. He turned the television on. He watched the picture bounce into focus. He turned the volume down. Cal still hadn't opened his eyes. He turned the volume down again. Maybe the kid was going to go back to sleep.

"I'm not going back to sleep. Don't worry."

"I'm not worried."

"I'm just resting."

Riley nodded. He put the remote down. He lay back on the bed and he watched the television. It was some kind of music show. Some girl, all dressed up and dancing around. It seemed weird for seven in the morning. Seven-thirty in the morning. Maybe it was supposed to be getting him pepped up for the day. Maybe it was the kind of thing he was supposed to be watching over the morning paper and a cup of coffee.

He stared at the screen. He thought the kid was sleeping, or something close to it. He turned the volume down again and he tried to breathe quiet. He willed the time to pass.

The girl was nearing the end of her routine. She was breathing hard. There was sweat on her forehead and her makeup was running. Riley never saw them looking like that on American television. People didn't sweat on American television. The television cut from the dancing and the sweat. It cut from the girl. It landed on a newscaster, sitting behind a big desk and staring straight into the camera. He blinked. She was reading words from a teleprompter. She was nodding but her eyes looked like they had no idea what the mouth below was saying. He couldn't even guess what she was talking about.

The dancing girl was back. They had mopped up the sweat and retouched the makeup. Then there was a cut to a commercial. Some kind of instant coffee drink. A woman was stirring coffee around in a mug with a spoon and smelling the steam coming off it. The colors were too bright. There were too many oranges and reds and the picture looked grainy, like it was coming apart in bits.

"Weird stuff, huh?" Cal's eyes were barely open. He blinked them slowly.

"Yeah."

"I used to love watching local television. It used to be the first thing I did when we checked into a motel. Turn on the television and check out the local channels. Helped me settle in. Helped me get used to a place."

They were silent.

"There used to be some crazy stuff on the Japanese channels."

"Well, it wasn't just the television."

"Yeah. Those were good times."

"You're making it sound like it was years back."

"Feels like it."

"It's been a year. A little less than a year."

"Has it? Feels longer."

They were quiet. They watched the television. Cal cleared his throat.

"You need some water?"

"No."

Cal stared up at the ceiling. Then he closed his eyes, and kept them closed.

"It was funny. When I was out walking—" Cal stopped.

"Yeah?"

"I just thought—maybe I'll keep walking. Maybe I'll just keep walking, and see what happens."

Riley turned and looked at Cal. The kid was still lying there with his eyes closed. Riley waited. Cal didn't say anything more. Riley turned back to the television. He looked at the screen. He guessed the news was over. They were watching some kind of game show. Cal's eyes were open now and he was watching the television. His eyes were glazed. Riley clicked the television off. He sat up. He cleared his throat.

"Kid."

"Yeah?"

"We don't have to do this."

Cal closed his eyes. Riley watched him.

"If you don't want to, we don't have to do this. There's no reason."

"It's too late."

"It's not too late."

"When I was out walking, I saw the posters. They're all over the place."

"It's not too late. There's always a way out. You coulda got an injury in practice."

Cal opened his eyes. He shook his head. "I coulda got an injury—"

"Or something."

"The doctors already cleared me."

"Sure."

"People don't get injuries the day before a fight."

"I'm just saying. If you don't want to fight you don't have to. You don't have to do anything you don't want to do."

"I know."

"I know how sometimes other people can make decisions for you. I mean, other people can push you into doing something maybe you wouldn't do otherwise."

"Sure."

Riley paused. He shook his head. He tried to think of a way of putting it. He leaned forward and then he spoke.

"You don't owe anyone. You don't owe me. That's what I'm trying to say. You don't owe me."

He looked at Cal. Cal was silent. He swung his legs down and sat up on the bed.

"It's not like that."

He looked at Riley. He leaned forward so his weight was resting on his hands.

"I don't know anything else."

Riley nodded. Cal looked at him.

"I'm not good at anything. Fighting's the only thing I've ever been good at."

Riley looked down at his hands. He swallowed.

"You know? It's the only thing."

He looked up. He looked at the kid. He didn't say anything. There was nothing he could say. The decision was Cal's. It didn't belong to anyone else. That was something he should have known. The game wasn't about options. It didn't keep things open, or leave ways out.

It closed things down. In the end it closed everything down. He shut his eyes. Things would have to play out. There was no other way. Things had been playing out for a long time. Cal knew that. He thought about it and it was like the kid had always known that. It was like the kid had understood something about the game he was only starting to learn now.

It wasn't his. He opened his eyes. He felt Cal beside him and it was like he saw it. All the things he couldn't stop, and everything he couldn't control. He guessed the feeling stretched that far. He guessed he'd say it did. He looked down at his hands. They were steady as they rested on his legs. He stood up.

"Come on. Let's get going. Enough of this."

"Okay."

"How about you take a shower and get that out of the way."

"Yeah."

Cal got up, more quickly this time. He went into the bathroom. Riley went over to the dresser and stood over the suitcases. He began selecting things, carefully. He lined the things up on the bed. He looked at the order of it.

He would pack it all up for Cal. He'd done it a hundred times. He would pack it all up and he would unpack it all when they arrived at the venue. He would prepare everything.

He could hear the sound of the shower running. He could hear the sound of the water hitting against the tub. It blinked in and out of focus as Cal moved. He could hear Cal moving—that was what he was hearing. He picked up a big duffel bag and unzipped it. He shook it open. He rolled up towels. He folded shorts and sweatshirts. He packed pads. He packed gloves. The shower kept running. He packed tape. He packed guards. It wouldn't take him long. He would be finished by the time Cal got out. He had been doing this a long time. He never forgot anything.

The shower had stopped. Riley heard the door open. When he turned Cal was standing in the doorway. He was leaning against the doorframe watching him.

"You showered?"

Cal nodded.

"Good."

He turned back and continued packing. He was almost finished. He threw in a couple of sports bottles. He left space for a few bottles of water. He did a last sort-through.

He picked out a pair of nail scissors. Some more tape. He hesitated for a second. His fingers moved across a wooden rosary. They closed around it. He moved back over to the bed.

Cal sat down on the other bed and watched him. Riley threw the things down. He unzipped the side pockets. He slid things in. He lifted the edges of the bag to shake the contents down, moving his hands through and patting things into place. A minute passed. He zipped the bag up.

"I'm gonna go out and get some bottles of water."

"Okay."

"Or maybe I'll get it while we're out for breakfast."

Cal shrugged. "Okay."

"I'm just thinking aloud."

He stood with his hands on his waist and looked at Cal. "I'll get it while we're out for breakfast. That's easier."

"Okay."

He checked the time. "You hungry?"

"Sure."

"You're on late, so you can eat normal."

"Yeah."

They stood alone in the room, the two of them together. They looked at the bag on the bed. There was nothing to do. There were hours until the fight. Riley listened to the sound of the tap dripping in the bathroom. He listened and he shook his head. Now the dead time started. Now there was nothing to do but wait.

10

They headed to the Caliente around two. It took them half an hour. Normally it would take them ten minutes. Less. Normally it would take them five minutes. Today it took them half an hour. They had to keep stopping. It was fight day. The town was buzzing. The street was buzzing. Even the motel was buzzing. Cal didn't think the motel could buzz, but today it was buzzing. He stepped out of the room and he felt it right away.

There were people everywhere. The area around the check-in desk was knee-deep in fighters. Fighters and trainers and hangers-on. The teams were big. They took up space. They filled up the lobby. Everywhere he looked there was someone new. Someone else to say hey to. It took them ten minutes, just to get down the stairs and into the lobby. And that was just saying hey. That was without stopping to talk.

They gave up on moving and stood in the lobby. Riley did the talking. Riley always did the talking. He could work a room in no time flat if he needed to. He could check in with every guy he needed to check in with, he could say hey where he needed to say hey, and he could walk out leaving every guy he talked to feeling special. Years in the game and he had it down to a science.

Cal let him do his thing. He waited. They would get to the hall. They would settle in. He tried to shake out the drifting in his head. He tried to get his head to focus.

Riley turned to him. "You ready?"

He nodded.

They walked out.

"Cal. Riley."

They looked up.

"Brett."

"You guys heading over?"

"Yeah. Just heading over now."

"A lot of guys there already."

"I guess the doors open at 4:30. Card starts at 5:30."

"Yeah. Early, huh?"

"Hey, they do things different down here. They leave lots of drinking time for after."

"Guess so. See you guys over there."

They nodded and started walking again. The crowd had thinned out. A couple guys to nod hey to, and that was it. Cal kept his head down. It wouldn't be long now. The fight was almost here. He wanted for it to be now. He was tired of the waiting. He couldn't keep it up anymore. He knew it was only a few hours but the time slowed down in the final hours. It slowed down like it was thinking about stopping altogether.

It never actually stopped. It just took its fucking time. It took its fucking time till you were just about ready to give up.

"Kid? We're here."

He looked up. They were at the Caliente. There were fans everywhere. They came up carrying things in their hands. Pictures. Programs. T-shirts. Just all kinds of things.

Cal stopped. He had time for the fans. All fighters had time for the fans. It wasn't about vanity or ego. The fans *saw* the fighters. They saw them the way they really were, in the ring. They reminded them of what they were capable of doing. Before a fight, the fans were just about the best thing coming.

They came up and surrounded him. There were more of them than he thought. They felt like more, crammed right up against him. He signed things. He said hey. He posed for pictures. Riley stayed by his side. He didn't move an inch. He would be in all the pictures, glaring at the camera. Riley hated this stuff, but he knew how it was important. He knew what it did for a fighter.

When they started asking for autographs for their friends, Riley motioned that time was up. Cal nodded. He started moving. He left Riley to wrap things up. The fans moved away. They knew the rules. They were there and then they were gone. Cal turned his head to look back at them. They were already waiting for the next guy. He shook his head.

They walked to the side door of the Caliente. The same one they had used yesterday, he recognized it. They stopped just outside. Neither of them moved to open it. They just looked at it.

"So this is it."

"Yeah."

"Well."

They should have had some kind of ritual. A handshake or a huddle or a prayer—they should have had something to do. They stood a beat too long. Then Riley wrenched the door open.

The door blew back. It blew open like there was more behind it than just air. It almost knocked Riley back a step or two; he had to brace his feet to steady the door. Cal stared at the air pouring out. It felt thick and dense like normal air wasn't. It had a feeling like normal air didn't. This air, it just came pouring out of the doorway.

"Fucking air-conditioning."

"Yeah."

"Go on in."

They stepped through the door. Riley was right. The air-conditioning was on too strong. Cal shivered. They kept moving down the corridor. Riley was already yanking his duffel bag open and pulling out a hoodie. He threw it over Cal's shoulders. Cal nodded thanks. They kept moving. Riley reached a hand over and pulled the hoodie close. Cal pushed his arms through and zipped it up. They turned the corner and followed the signs for the dressing rooms.

They kept following the signs until they came to a door with his name on it. It was just a piece of paper taped to the wall but it still made him look. He looked at Riley and he shrugged. They stepped inside.

Riley set the duffel bag down and looked around the room. It was big enough to accommodate a team. Say three or four guys plus a couple hangers-on. There were benches and chairs. A few mats were propped up against the wall. There was room for stretching. There was room for hitting pads and there was even room for a bit of light sparring. It wasn't what he expected. It would do. It was more than doing.

Riley sat down. He looked at Cal. The kid was just standing in the room. He wasn't looking around. He was just standing there.

"Not bad."

"No."

There was a television set up in the corner. Cal jerked his head toward it.

"Do you think we can watch the fights on that?"

"Looks like. They've probably got a live feed."

"I'd like to watch the fights."

Riley kept looking around the room. There was the television, and then parked down one side of the room there was a vanity table. It was flashy as hell—a rim of big light-bulbs and switches everywhere. He stood up and walked over. He stood in front of it. He looked at himself in the mirror. He straightened his posture.

"Take a look at this."

"Yeah."

He leaned over and flicked a couple switches. The lights flooded on. Riley squinted. Cal smiled. Riley looked at him through the mirror.

"Are you fucking kidding me?"

"That's to make sure I look pretty."

"Next thing you know they'll be expecting you to come out in a silk robe."

"I guess some guys might use it."

"Gray might use it. Henry—"

"Yeah. He'd use it."

"Does he come out in a robe?"

Riley shook his head. "Can't remember. But he's got some pretty fancy hair."

Riley switched the lights off. He turned around. He and Cal looked at each other.

"So."

"Yeah."

"What's the time?"

"Three-thirty."

"There's time still."

"There's a lot of time."

Cal still hadn't sat down.

"You planning on standing there for the next four hours?"

Cal shrugged.

"Okay." Riley cleared his throat. "I'm gonna go wander. Go see the lay of the land and all that."

"Okay."

"You wanna come?"

"No."

Riley looked around the room uneasily. He couldn't hear a thing. There had to be other people close by. There had to be other fighters, other teams, but he didn't hear anything.

"You shouldn't just stay here. Come on. We got time."

"I'm okay."

Riley shrugged. He jerked the door open.

"Won't be long."

Cal nodded. Riley looked at him again, and then he walked through the door. He heard it click shut behind him. He went outside. He walked around. Then he turned and headed back. It wasn't that he was worrying. There just wasn't that much to look at. There wasn't that much to do. He stood in the parking lot and then he turned around and came back because he couldn't think of anything else to do.

He went inside. He figured the doors had to be close to opening, because the place was littered with people. The corridors were bouncing with personnel. They had gone from empty to bouncing, just in the time he'd been wandering around outside. He stopped one of the staff.

"How long till the doors open?"

"About forty minutes."

Riley went back to the dressing room. He nodded to Cal.

"Not long now till they open the doors."

"What time is it?"

"I guess about 4:00."

It was still too early to be warming up. Sound from the hall was being piped into the room. Riley craned his neck. He listened to the sound. The doors must have opened. He could hear the hall filling up with people. He could feel the anticipation. Just in the noise of it.

Riley looked at Cal.

"So it's started."

The kid didn't say anything. He nodded. The sound kept building across the speakers. The hall wasn't that big and there couldn't be that many people in it now but the way the sound was amplifying it sounded like it was the Superdome filling up around them. Riley looked around uneasily and then sat down.

He looked at Cal. The kid didn't look distracted. He looked calm, and he was moving methodically as he began a series of lazy stretches. Like it had nothing to do with him, everything that was happening around the fight and everything that would happen inside the fight too. Riley knew he wouldn't be feeling that. He knew there was no way that was what he would be feeling inside. But from the outside that's how it looked was all.

It always happened. The fight stopped belonging to you. It started happening all around you and in some ways you had to disconnect. It was a big fucking machine. Once it started up it couldn't be stopped or even stalled. It just kept going. Riley looked around the room. Everything about it was already looking like it couldn't be changed. He took a deep breath.

They sat for another hour. Then they began warming up. Cal went through his stretches. His body was warm and supple and it didn't take much to loosen up the muscles. He kept his breathing slow and regular and he took his body through the routine. It took time. He had time. His mind went blank and after a while he just sank right into the feeling of the stretches. He worked until his body was loose. Then he stood up again.

He looked at Riley. He was slipping on mitts. The sparring would sharpen the muscles. First they were loosened. Then they were tightened. The tightening couldn't happen without the loosening. It was like there were two separate sets of muscles in the body. The first set was used doing ordinary things. Walking on the street. Sitting at the kitchen table. The other set was used in a fight. The rituals of stretching and warming up, they were just part of making sure the right set was in place before a fighter headed into the ring.

"You done?"

He nodded. Riley kicked the mat away. Cal slipped his sweatpants off. He tucked his shirt into his shorts and laced on gloves. Then he turned around. Riley was waiting.

He hit the pads. Riley held them dead center. He didn't move them. He didn't move apart from a step backward and then a step forward to recover position. The point wasn't to sharpen the reflexes. The point wasn't to adjust speed. The point was just to feel the power of the punch. The sound of each blow was deafening. Beneath it he could hear the fights running through the speakers. It sounded like a good crowd. It sounded like the card was playing well.

They switched to the legs. They worked the knees first. He held Riley in a clinch and he threw knees. His body felt good. He wasn't feeling the muscles at all. They moved into kicks. They started with low kicks. After a bit he moved up to the torso. He didn't need to shift his balance. He didn't even need to tune it. The snap on each kick was clean and good. His breath was coming a little heavier now and he was sweating through his T-shirt.

Riley nodded. "Okay." He tossed him a towel. Cal wiped the sweat off his face. He threw a sweatshirt over his shoulders.

There was a knock on the door and then the doctor walked in with a fight official. Cal pulled his gloves off. Riley came over and started taping up his hands. The doctor and the fight official watched. He did the left and then the right one. He handed Cal the four-ounce gloves he would use for the fight. Cal pulled them on. He pulled his fingers through, one by one. He laced them up and then he stood and waited as the doctor wrapped the tape around the wrists. He waited as the official signed them. They nodded and wished him a good fight and then they left.

He sat down, one leg propped up on a chair. He sat down facing the television. Riley switched it on. He pulled a chair up and sat down next to him.

They were well into the card now. Past the midway point. They would watch a couple fights. Then they would do the final warmup and head to the ring. Cal always watched the fights. He watched them because he was interested. He watched them because there was nothing else to do. Being with Riley, watching the fights—it was the only thing he could do. It took his mind off things but it kept him focused.

Cal looked at the screen. It was the tail end of a fight. He recognized one of the guys. He'd seen him fight, somewhere or other. The other guy looked like a fish. They rolled around a bit. Eventually the guy gave up and they settled into some good old-fashioned ground and pound. The fight was boring.

"You got some orange juice?"

Riley nodded and handed Cal the bottle. He took a sip. He swished it around in his mouth. He swallowed and waited for the next fight to come up.

"Who's next?"

"Dunno."

"Where are we on the card?"

"I think that was the sixth fight."

Cal nodded. He turned back to the television. The screen ran into a trailer. It ran into Rivera. It ran right up against him. The big punches. The big knockouts. The greatest moments. He watched like he'd never seen it before. He'd seen it all, but he watched like it was new.

Now he was watching some television presenter. The presenter talked fast. He talked like he believed in what he was saying. He said Cal was the only fighter to go the distance with Rivera. He said he was the only fighter Rivera hadn't knocked out cold. He said it was a rematch four years in the making and a dream for any fight fan. Rivera was out for revenge. Rivera was looking for the knockout. It would be Cal's chin against Rivera's knockout power. That's what he said.

The screen cut to Rivera. He stood in his dressing room. The presenter asked him his prediction for the fight.

"Knockout."

"A knockout in the first? In the second? What's your prediction?"

He shrugged.

"I will knock him out."

He didn't say anything else. Cal exhaled, slowly. He could feel Riley standing behind him, watching the screen. He clapped his hand against Cal's shoulder and then he left it there. He pressed his fingers into his skin.

"What a bunch of bullshit."

"I always forget that they put that crap in."

"Yeah, well don't forget that's exactly what it is. A bunch of crap."

He nodded. He couldn't think about it. He couldn't think about the possibility of a knockout. He didn't know what that was like. He couldn't carry that into the ring with him. The next fight was starting up. It was a Top Team fighter, some guy he'd never seen. Young. Riley leaned closer to the screen.

"We saw that kid yesterday."

"Yeah?"

"Yeah. Kid's something."

"Who's he fighting?"

"Dixon."

Cal nodded. He watched the kid and tried to clear his head. The kid had a nice physique. Everything looked natural. He didn't have a six-pack and he had a bit of puppy fat around the middle but his muscles were nice and long and he carried them easy. The kid wouldn't gas. Just looking Cal knew he wouldn't gas.

The ref called them to the center of the ring. The kid didn't look at Dixon through the instructions. He bounced his shoulders. He rolled out his neck. Dixon stared at him. You couldn't stare down a guy who wasn't looking at you. Dixon's face was turning sour. He held out his gloves for the touch. He held them out like he thought the kid was going to refuse them.

They went back to their corners. The kid continued with the neck rolls. He stretched out his calves. He put his hands on the ropes and he stretched out his arms. He continued with the bouncing. He was still bouncing when the bell rang.

The bell rang and the kid burst out of the corner. The bouncing led right into it. He raced forward. He closed the distance. He *flew*. He used flying kicks and flying knees to close the distance. He whipped the body up and the leg out. He swung the arms tight for velocity. His technique was perfect. His form was perfect.

Cal had never seen anything like it in his life. The kid landed into a one-two combination. He aimed for the head. Ten seconds into the fight and he was aiming for the head. The kid didn't waste time. He transitioned like it was nothing. He moved so fast and so pretty it was hard to remember there was another guy in the ring.

Cal looked in the ring for Dixon. He had to look hard. The guy wasn't doing anything. The guy was barely in the fight. The kid kept pressing the action. The kid kept making the fight. He threw a kick, from the ground this time. Cal could see Dixon's eyes close to the blow. He could see the sweat fly off his head. The kid didn't stop to admire.

Everybody in the stadium was admiring but the kid wasn't stopping for it. He locked his hands around Dixon's neck.

Cal couldn't count the seconds before the knees began. The kid was balancing on the ball of his foot. He was purchasing an extra two, three inches to hit the head. He stood high on the ball of his foot and he leaned into the knee. He put the whole of his weight behind it. He landed two solid knees to the jaw and then he let go. He jumped away and bounced back into position, hands up. Dixon lurched across the ring, body bent in two. Cal leaned forward.

"He's got some busted-up ribs."

Riley squinted at the screen. Dixon was holding one side of his torso. He was saying something to his corner. His mouth was open and he wasn't even looking for the fight. The fight was right in front of him. He was talking to his corner like it was just practice, but the fight was right there in front of him.

The kid got on him again. He backed him up like it was nothing. Dixon fell into the corner. Five, six punches and he was slumping against the ropes. He was falling to the canvas.

The kid gave up on the punches. He started dropping stomps. Dixon's head banged hard against the post. He was bleeding everywhere. He was making a mess all over the canvas. The kid swung his leg up and around to get extra force. He jumped up light, like it was nothing. The stomp landed so hard the guys sitting ringside winced. Guys didn't wince too often, but they were all wincing. The ref waved his hands in the air. He slid in to end the fight.

The kid stepped away from Dixon. He stepped away casual. He was breathing light. He looked around like he was wondering what happened next. He smiled at someone in the crowd. He half-waved. Cal stared at the screen. He shook his head.

There was a knock at the door.

"Ten minutes." Then footsteps falling away.

They didn't move. They didn't look at each other. It was okay. Everything would follow. The time had gone. From here he would just follow on the current of what was happening. It happened to him. He just had to follow along. They stood up. Riley snapped the television off. He slipped on gloves, without speaking. They started moving. They started sparring, nice and tight. They started sparring, immediately.

They would go through the final circuit. They would do the final bit of sparring. They would move, across the room, doing more than just sparring, doing more than just warming the body up. They would take the body through its final preparation. They would get the reflexes ready. They would get the heart racing and the mind pumping so that everything just ran into the fight.

They gathered momentum. They moved fast. They hit hard.

"Five minutes."

These were the last moments alone. He didn't notice them, usually. There was too much going on around the fight. Too many people. Too much anticipation. But this time he noticed them. He stared at Riley and he counted through them slow. He breathed out. Riley looked at him and he nodded. He clapped him on the back.

Last knock. It was time. Riley grabbed the pail. He grabbed the towel. He looked at Cal. They stood up and left the dressing room. They followed the guy down the corridors. They came out into the holding space. They were told to wait. They waited.

The music was playing loud as the fighters from the previous match exited the hall. It must have been a short fight. They stood there and waited. Cal looked at Riley. His face was bare to the light. It was tired and gaunt. He looked old. Cal had never seen him looking so old.

Cal nudged him. He tried to smile at him when he turned his head. It wasn't much of a smile but he tried. Riley nodded and then he turned his head forward again. The guy grabbed Cal's arm. He counted down from five on his fingers. He directed them forward through the entrance.

They walked up into the entrance. It was pitch black and curtained off. The entrance music came on. It pumped through ten-foot speakers. The lights were flashing right into his face. They told him to step onto the platform. Riley had disappeared. There was smoke everywhere and it was like the platform was just disappearing right into it. Cal couldn't see the edges in front of him. Maybe the edges weren't there. If he moved he might fall all the way down. The platform was moving. He couldn't help but look down. He saw the fans. Their mouths were open and they were screaming but he couldn't hear anything.

The platform hit the runway. It hit it with a bump. He felt his knees buckle. They almost gave way but didn't.

His insides were rising up in his throat. His head was spinning. He was getting turned inside out. His eyes were watering from the smoke and he wasn't hearing so good. The music was too loud. The fans were too loud. He couldn't hear them but he knew they were too loud.

He felt a hand on his shoulder. It propelled him forward and down the runway. It took him out of the smoke. It took him away from the music. Everything started clearing up. His heart was still pumping but he heard the pumping in his ears like normal, not like some outside press of noise and smoke and movement. Riley kept pushing him forward. He kept the hand there. He kept the pressure there. He let him go when he had cleared the gap.

Cal stepped out ahead of him. He made his way to the ring. The ring was glowing clear and hard. He looked at it. The canvas was so white it was blinding. For a moment he didn't see anything but the ring. The people around fell silent. They fell out of focus. He looked at the ring. The fuzziness left the picture. He could see now. In an instant it had become clear. He stepped off the runway and walked around the ring. He climbed through the ropes. Then the noise came back.

11

He stood in the corner. He looked up to the lights. Stadium lights—they just blew the vision out. They just turned everything into white. The white only stopped where it was tinged with black. It was like temporary blindness, before everything curtained into dark.

He looked at the whiteness. He listened to the noise of the crowd. He could hear every sound they made like they were inside him. He heard them inside like he would never be alone again.

He lowered his head. The stadium lights fell onto his neck. The light just poured down onto him. He could feel it falling. He could feel it like he was seeing it in particles. They were getting into his eyes, like dust. He kept having to blink his eyes to keep them out. He lowered his head further. He lowered it so that his chin was driving right down into his chest.

His head was light. His body was light. It was the detail

that was doing it. Everywhere there was detail. He placed his hands on the ropes. The grain of the rope, each individual piece of ribbing—just the touch was enough to burn him. His toe brushed against the canvas, and he felt the give of the floor against the tug of the nail. It wasn't just the rope and canvas. He could feel the detail in everything.

He could see everything. He could hear everything, he could hear the guy in the right tier, leaning forward to pick up his beer. He could hear the kid sitting ringside, flapping his program up and down on his knee. Everywhere there was detail. The detail was setting him apart from where he was. It was pushing him close. Too close to see where he really was, and what he was really doing—

Riley caught him by the neck. He pulled his head toward his chest. He pressed his mouth against his ear. He cupped his hand around his neck. He rubbed him down. He worked the tendons, with his fingers, with his thumb. He moved his hand up and around the head. He rubbed hard into the hair, with his fingers. He moved his hand back down into the neck. He slapped the neck, he slapped the shoulders. He worked his fingers across the shoulders. He moved them back to the neck.

The whole time he was talking to him. Just a stream of talk, the words slipping into his ear and then out again. He kept the hand moving as he talked. The words slipped into the hand. The hand slipped into the words.

You keep it standing as long as you can and then you just take him down. Take him right down, before he takes you

*down. You wear him down. This is your fight. Don't you forget
that. This is your fight. You can make this your fight. You just
fight smart and you fight to go the distance. Sure this fight is
gonna go the distance, and at the end of the fight you're gonna
show the judges that you've done enough to get the win. Wear
him down. You just keep wearing him down—*

He wasn't hearing the words. It was just more sound,
washing down over him. His mouth fell open. The dry-
ness rushed in. He felt the hand, squeezing at the back of
his neck. Riley kept talking. Riley kept working the hand.

*You can win this. You've fought this guy before. You know
what makes him tick. You know how he works. That's the
advantage. Don't forget that. He's not gonna surprise you.
You're the one who's gonna do the surprising. You've got all the
tools to take him apart. You've got everything you need to take
him to pieces. You've got some solid takedowns. Those are
gonna be key. Those are gonna win this fight for you. Don't get
fancy. Don't get cute. Just take him down quick. Just use your
wrestling and your ground and pound and you can win this.
You can wear him down—*

He nodded. It didn't mean anything. Riley knew it didn't
mean anything. He knew the game plan wasn't going to
work. They both knew it. That wasn't the point. The point
wasn't about a game plan. It wasn't about what he said. He
could have been saying anything and it would have had the
same effect. He was just birthing him into the fight. It was
a physical thing. It was a thing about touch, about the
closeness of the mouth to the ear, it was a thing about the

feeling of sound hitting against the eardrum, the heat of human breath—

He shook his head free. Riley's hand fell back. He stood for a moment, alone. It would begin when it began. He knew he'd find himself in it soon enough. There wasn't any stopping it now.

He turned to center. He turned to look at Rivera. Corner to corner, he looked at Rivera.

He was standing with his head down and his back turned to the ring and then his back just stopped moving. As if he felt Cal watching. It froze like it wasn't part of something living. The moment was long. Then the back moved again, a slow ripple running from the shoulders down to the base of the spine.

Rivera turned his head. He turned it slow. He turned and he looked, from one eye. Just one. He looked at Cal, from that one eye, from over his shoulder, from the quarter cut of his face. They stood across the ring from each other. They looked. Then Rivera swung his head back down again.

Rivera standing across from him in the ring. Twenty feet and sixty seconds away. Less—less than that already. Already the seconds were counting backward. Cal sucked the breath into his mouth and he pushed it back down his throat. His heart was pumping. In his mouth and in his stomach. It cleared the distance in no time flat. He could feel his body pulsing. Like every part of him was throbbing. Like his pulse was everywhere at once.

The snap of the elastic in the trunks. The sound of spit hitting against the side of the pail. The turtle curl of flesh in the back of the neck. He might never see things so clearly. Where he was standing now, with everything so clear—he would spend the rest of the fight trying to get back here. He stared across the ring. Things changed without moving. Nothing moved, but the picture was already different and the fight was that much closer.

The ref walked to the center of the ring. His movements were neat and clean. The crease in his trousers was clean. The collar of his shirt was clean. He was clean, every part of him was clean. Cal saw him walk forward, from the corner of his eye. He saw him cross himself quick. Pray for a good fight. Pray for a clean fight. A downward-sideways flash of the hand as he walked. He stopped dead center. He motioned them forward. He did not look at them but he motioned them forward.

They walked forward. In the end all it took was steps to cross the distance. The distance fell away easy. Like it was nothing real. Like it was nothing solid. He did not think, now I am walking into this, now it is beginning. He missed the thought. His legs were walking but already his mind had moved on. Already it was somewhere else, so that he missed the threshold of the fight. He walked forward and he found himself in it. No bell rang out. No boundary was crossed. But the fight had started.

The staredown snapped through the air. It bounced across the ring. Rivera was pushing it out as he walked.

Pushing it with all the force in his body. In the hard chop of his walk, in the bouncing of his chest, in the shoulders riding high and in the eyes—in the pure clean madness of the eyes. The eyes were hollow and flat and that was where the madness of the staredown was. Cal felt the staredown like a physical thing, coming toward him and out of him too. It built as they walked toward each other. It accelerated like it was heading for a collision.

They met at the center. Like it was magnetic. Like the switch had been thrown and the circuit laid down. He couldn't blink out of it. Neither of them could. It had grabbed hold and it wouldn't let go. It had started and now they had to see it through. There was nothing beyond them in the fight. There were no tools. There was no ball, no goal, no base. There was nothing but air and intention. The two fighters made the fight. Together they had to make it real.

The ref rolled the fight forward. He stated the rules. He asked Rivera if he was ready. He asked Cal if he was ready. Cal missed the asking. He didn't hear it. The ref pointed his finger at his chest. He asked him again if he was ready. He jerked his head yes. The ref clapped his hands together and sent them back to their corners. They didn't touch gloves. There was no physical contact.

They retreated to their corners. They backed into them and they didn't break the stare. Cal knew they wouldn't break it until one of them took a solid hit. The kind of hit you closed your eyes to. You would open them after. You would look back again. You would look back into the eyes, you had to. But the way you looked at a guy who had hurt you was different. The hurting made it different. The fight would be somewhere new. Cal already knew the fight would take no breaks. It would just move, and then keep moving, and then move again.

Every fight was new. He had to remember that. Cross into the fight and the view, it changed. The eyes got moved around. The vision shifted. There was no preparing for a fight. Not really. Nothing repeated. Nothing became the same again, and nothing was written—

The bell. They sprang forward. The bell was still ringing in his ears and he was two yards forward into the fight. He cleared the ring, light on his feet, feet moving so fast it had to be the nervousness, feet carrying him forward through the side to side. Side and side and then the other side—his feet were moving on their own. There was no thought running from the brain down to the feet, there was nothing but the feet moving. His body surfed and floated on the current of his feet and his eyes watched Rivera surge straight forward. Pure counterpoint. They were working in pure counterpoint. He was moving from side to side while Rivera moved forward like a cut.

They arrived at the same time. They met dead center. They sprang back. Like they had collided and ricocheted away. They still hadn't touched. They eyed each other. They eyed each other as they circled and then they circled again.

The looking changed. Its temperature did. Cal was seeing things in it now. He was seeing things in Rivera. He was seeing caution and he also thought he was seeing rage. Right at the back of the eyes. It was tempered by the caution and it was breeding it too. Rivera never allowed for rage without caution. He was too cunning for that. That was everything key about Rivera. The caution and the cunning and the raging. He could see it in him, right in the eyes and all the way back.

His feet were still dancing. Rivera kept circling. They were feeling each other out, in the ritual performed by one good fighter matched against another good fighter. They measured the body's stance, the quickness of reflex and steadiness of eye. They read intensities of focus and intention. They read for holes in concentration. The opening moments were crucial.

Rivera hung close to the ground. Like he was tamping down the power of his body. Like the weight would coil and compress it before release. He would suddenly erupt into movement. He was just waiting to launch himself. Cal kept dancing, as if the movement would keep Rivera still. He danced in and then he danced away again. In and away. He felt Rivera's attention flinch at the speed of his moving. He felt his eye flick down to the feet and then back up to the eyes. He kept dancing. His eyes never left Rivera's face.

The time was passing. The opening minute would pass and they would still be stuck in the gate. Fighters got stuck here all the time. They got stuck here so long that they awoke to the expectation of the crowd, the impatience of the referee. They got stuck here so long they got pulled out of the fight.

They flung themselves at each other. It was like the thought and the impulse was shared. Velocity thrust against velocity—the collision was worse than vertigo. Nothing landed. Just a tangle of knees and elbows and forearms. Heads brushed close against heads. Cal's chest slammed hard against Rivera's. For a moment he felt heartbeat against heartbeat. Then he flung him off and they both backed away.

They looked at each other, warily. He bounced on his feet. The ring vibrated with the weight of the bouncing. It surprised him. He forgot his own size. He forgot how large he was. How much larger he was than anything that was normal. They both were. Everything was amplified by the size of their bodies. Things happened fast when you were this big. Things ended in an instant. Faster than you meant. You could knock a guy out without meaning to.

Form imposed itself on the fight. Rivera surged forward with a left. Cal saw it coming early. He flicked his head back and threw a right counter. Rivera saw it coming early. They canceled each other out. They backed away again.

It looked like nothing had changed. It looked like the fight had gone nowhere and like the slate was still clean. It showed how little of the fight could be seen, from the outside. Inside that instant they had been evenly matched. They had read each other perfectly. The fight became infinitely longer in that exchange.

They returned to the circling. They were both bouncing now. They were moving their hands fast. Their heads, their feet—everything moved. The agitation was out in the air now. Rivera came forward, lead leg tapping hard at the canvas. He retreated again. Cal started forward, and then stopped. At the same moment they both tucked their chins in further.

Rivera threw a low kick. It carved through the air. It sang out. It smacked as it landed.

It made the first hit of the fight. It slowed everything down. Cal could feel his heartbeat slowing. He could see his leg shiver in slow motion. Then the force of the contact whipped through fast and surged into pain. He bit into his mouthguard and willed himself to focus past it. He stood on the leg. He didn't take his eyes off Rivera's face. He kept his hands up. The whole time he kept his hands up.

Rivera launched a solid right-left leading into a knee. A textbook Rivera combination. Cal read it in his eyes as he approached. He tucked in his elbows and he protected the head. He fended off the punches with his gloves. He waited a beat and then he shifted his torso away from the knee. The knee flew past him into the air.

He threw a left counter, right down the middle. It grazed against Rivera's chin. He saw his skin shiver with the blow. They both fell back. They looked at each other. He heard the thudding in his ears again. He looked at Rivera and he watched the tightness in the eyes. He waited for it to flicker. He didn't expect holes. He just wanted a flicker. He just wanted it to give way, a little.

Rivera threw a high kick this time. It came fast. It came fast, but Cal read it coming. It smacked against his forearm. Cal threw a big overhand right. Rivera dodged and countered with a left hook. He threw wide. Cal moved in. He got him into a clinch. He locked it in. He looked for the takedown. He shifted the shoulders. He used his weight. Rivera threw a knee. Cal pulled him closer so there wasn't room for kneeing. He shut him down—it felt good, the shutting down. Rivera started chopping away at the head. He reached up and he held the neck with one hand and he chopped away at the head.

Cal let go of the bodylock and he blocked the shots. Rivera switched to the body. Cal kept his hands caged around the head and he lowered his elbows. Rivera kept kneeing him. He hit him below the elbows. Cal felt the blows go shuddering past the elbows and into the body. Just the feel of it was enough to make him gasp. He lowered his hands and then he threw an uppercut. The uppercut landed. He felt Rivera's body loosen and then tighten, immediately. Rivera would go in for the takedown next. He saw it like the idea was being telegraphed to him—

Cal sprawled fast, almost before Rivera shot in. They crashed against each other, Rivera down below and Cal slumped over on top. He fumbled to get hold of him. He struggled to lock his arms around his chest. He felt Rivera's head thudding against his shoulder. It pushed hard against his throat and he almost gagged from the pressure. Right inside his mouth. The throat tightened all the way up to the mouth. He closed his eyes and he swallowed to push the feeling back down.

They flung each other off. The separation ripped through the ring. They landed on their feet and stood several feet apart. Neither of them moved. He looked at Rivera. The smell of him was still up in his nose. He kept looking at him. He looked into his eyes and then he tried to read what would come next. He tried to prepare himself.

Rivera threw a big overhand right. It hit him on the chin. It sent everything wobbling. He reached out and grabbed him back into the clinch. Rivera threw him off. He tossed him against the ropes. He threw another big right. He bounced straight into it. He bounced off the ropes and straight into the right, like he was trying to meet him halfway.

The sound of the second punch just carved through the air. It sounded like somebody had taken a baseball bat to his head. Get hit like that and the body walked away from the fight. He thought he had remembered how hard Rivera hit. He had remembered nothing. The mind didn't remember that kind of feeling. The mind was conditioned to forget. Everything about the mind and the body was conditioned to forget.

The punch ripped a hole into the fight. It cut off the air. It was like his head was coming apart. His legs gave out on him for real and he fell down to one knee. Like the scene had gone romantic and he was proposing marriage. Rivera started kneeing him in the head. He took the first knee. His head fell back and his body swayed. He took a few more knees and then he staggered back to his feet.

As he stood up, Rivera kicked him in the head from standing. A solid soccer kick. It just about knocked his head off. It didn't hurt. It just knocked his head off. He looked up at Rivera. He tried to get the breathing back into his chest. Rivera threw another kick. This one went to the thigh. It sang out as it landed. Rivera was feeding off the singing. Cal could tell. The next kick crashed into his side and he felt his lung gasp. Like the air had burst right out of it.

He felt Rivera follow up. There were maybe two or three punches—he wasn't able to count them. They blurred into each other. It was all just impact. He shook his head awake. He forced his mind to focus until the punches became distinct. Until he could count them one by one. There was no air for him to breathe and it made the focusing hard. It felt like someone had sucked all the oxygen out of the place.

His chest clenched. He coughed and tasted blood. Rivera surged against him again. Now he moved into the clinch. Cal felt his hands lock around his neck and knew the knees would start next. He knew the idea, but only like it was far away. He wasn't sure when the knees began. He could see Rivera's leg working like a piston but he didn't feel the knees. He swayed with the blows. He counted them. He clung to Rivera. He tried to keep his footing and he tried to neutralize and he concentrated on counting the knees.

Rivera flung him off. He backed away several feet. He looked at Cal. He was breathing heavy in the mouth and his eyes were black. He shook his head in frustration and spat on the canvas. Cal watched him. He knew he should have been out. He knew he shouldn't be standing. It didn't make sense. The idea was still with him when Rivera came forward again.

It was like a wall running into him. He pushed against it. He tried to carve a space out for himself. Rivera kept moving forward. The blows were landing. The hooks and straights and knees and kicks—everything was landing. He felt the shape and size of each blow but he didn't feel the impact. He couldn't remember. He couldn't think. He knew the punches were landing but his legs still felt strong and his breathing was regular.

Rivera kept working. He knew Rivera. He knew he wasn't saving. He knew he was throwing everything. It was everything but none of it was reaching him. Just none of it was. Rivera drummed into his body. Five, six blows. He heard them but he didn't feel anything. He backed away from the blows. Rivera followed up. He threw into the head so that Cal felt his neck snapping and his chin bobbing. He pulled his chin down and he looked at Rivera. They looked at each other.

Rivera threw a big right. It landed square. Cal nodded into the blow and for a moment his knees buckled. Then the feeling passed and he was still standing. He looked at Rivera. They looked at each other. He couldn't knock him out. They both saw it. Rivera bounced on his feet and then he turned and walked away. He turned his back on him, in the ring. He walked away and Cal saw the frustration ripple off his body.

Somewhere in the distance he heard the announcer call thirty seconds. Only thirty seconds more. Rivera turned with the sound of the announcement. He rushed Cal. He grabbed hold of his head and he got in close. He threw and then he threw again. He followed punches with knees and knees with punches. Cal's chest went tight. He felt his legs and for the first time he felt the bruising in them. Something snapped and he wondered if his ribs had gone. He felt himself get caught in the question. He saw that his mind was drifting. He tried to make himself concentrate. His vision was blurring and his breath was coming short.

The bell rang. Rivera turned and retreated to his corner.

Cal stood in the center of the ring. The ref led him to the corner. He turned and nodded thanks. Riley jumped up through the ropes. He set down the stool. Cal collapsed onto it. His legs gave out on him. Riley fumbled inside his mouth for the guard. He closed his eyes. He heard his breath crashing in and out. There was music playing and there were people talking to him but he couldn't hear anything but the sound of his own breathing. He closed his eyes.

Riley looked at the kid. He was hurt, bad. The bruises on his legs were turning purple. They were six or seven inches wide, all down one side of his leg. His ribs were cracked or broken. Everything inside the body was battered. He was breathing ragged and his face was just a mess. He reached up and he placed his fingers on either side of his nose and he snapped it into place. He wiped up the blood. There were doctors crowding the corner. He looked at the kid. He looked at him and then he moved back for the doctors. He shook his head.

Cal reached a hand up to touch his nose. He couldn't remember at what point it had gone. His fingers dabbled at blood—he guessed there must be cuts. Riley moved a hand up to his face. Gently, he pushed Cal's hand away. Cal felt him peel his right eye open. He guessed it must have swollen shut. He hadn't even missed the vision. Riley said something to him. He couldn't hear him but he could tell he was saying something to him. He struggled to listen. He would always listen when Riley was talking to him. He leaned forward.

"You're hurt pretty bad, kid."

He nodded. He leaned back into the post. He concentrated on breathing.

"You want to stop?"

He didn't look at Riley.

"If you want to stop we stop."

He struggled to sit up in the corner. His legs were pretty weak. He couldn't feel them anymore. He kept trying to sit up, but it was hard.

"He opened up some nasty cuts. I don't know how long we can keep them closed. We got the doctors here—" Riley turned and looked at the doctors. He turned back to Cal. "We got the doctors here."

Cal pulled himself up. It was the lower back. He was slumped so far down his lower back was just laid out on the stool. He needed the legs to push him back up. Once he got his back up he'd be fine. He gripped the ropes with his hands. He pulled, hard.

"You went one long round with him. You did good. It's just not your day."

Cal drew his legs closer to the stool. He drew them in until they rested by the feet of the stool. He leaned forward. He grabbed hold of the ropes again. He paused for breath. He stared at the floor. He kept staring at the floor. Then he shook his head and he looked at Riley.

"He can't knock me out."

"What?"

"I said. He can't knock me out."

Riley shook his head.

"You can't fight, kid. You're all mashed up. I don't even know if the doctors are gonna clear you to fight. I say we call it a day. Call it quits and walk out of here with your dignity intact."

"He said he was gonna knock me out. He said it was gonna be a knockout."

"There's more to life than not getting knocked out, kid."

Cal didn't respond.

"There's more to life than proving him wrong."

Cal shook his head. He kept shaking it and then he swung himself up to his feet. He was standing. He swayed on his feet. Riley sprang up to hold him. He held him from behind, by the armpits like a sling. Cal stood for a few moments and recovered. Riley stood behind him. He held him, tight.

"Don't make me throw the towel in on this. Come on, kid. Don't make me do it."

Cal was breathing heavy. He could feel Riley's chest shaking with his weight. He felt his arms tighten again. He felt his hand brushing across his forehead. He swallowed.

"Let me do this."

"No."

"Let me do this."

"I couldn't live with it, Cal."

Cal reached a hand up. He patted Riley's arm. He patted, down the forearm and up again. He stopped. He rested his hand on his shoulder.

"Sure you can."

Cal let his hand drop. He stepped forward. He stood, on his own. He looked across the ring. It looked huge. He'd never seen it looking so huge in his life.

Rivera was standing in his corner. He was fresh, untouched.

Cal took a step forward. Riley followed then fell back again. He stared at Cal. He stared at him standing by himself in the ring and he didn't think he could do it. He didn't think he could sit back and watch. He could do anything for the kid but not that. Cal took another step forward. He wasn't steady on his feet and Riley saw that his legs were trembling.

He looked at the kid and it was like he felt something ripping apart inside him. It was never going to be done. It was falling apart around him but it was never going to be done. The pain of it was more than anything he had known. He stared at Cal and it was like he had known him forever. It was like the kid had always been standing in front of him.

He lowered his head. To watch, and keep watching, until it was over. He hadn't known it, but that had always been the pledge. That had been the promise. He raised his head. He looked at Cal. He kept looking at him, and he felt his throat swelling so that he could hardly breathe. He turned and stepped through the ropes. He dropped down into the corner. He stood for a second. Then he lifted his head, and he looked into the ring.

Cal stood in front of his corner. He looked up at the lights, one last time. From the corner of his eye he saw the ref motioning them forward. He coughed—the salty taste of blood rushed up against his tongue. His knees buckled under him. They swayed backward and then forward—his legs were weaker than he thought. He looked up again. The crowd became louder than before. He found himself saying a prayer.

The bell rang in two more rounds and it was finished. Rivera won by unanimous decision. Cal was still standing. He didn't look human by the end of it. His face was just a blur of flesh and blood and bone. There were no features in it. He stood in the ring and he listened as they announced Rivera's name. He leaned in to shake hands, and he felt the double clasp of Rivera's hands as he did it.

He backed away. He stepped through the ropes; his footing was unsteady and he almost fell as he did. Riley reached in to catch him. He guided him through the ropes. He wrapped his arm close around his shoulders and he held him up. He threw a towel over his head. He pulled it down over his face, and the towel went red with blood.

"It's over, kid," he said. "It's over."

Cal nodded, head covered. Riley held him up, body pressed close, and guided him forward. They moved slowly, step by step. Cal felt his legs give and he stopped. He stood, breathing heavy. Riley stood with him. He waited until he recovered, and then they began moving again.

Cal could hear the crowd applaud as they walked. He heard it as though it were very far away. A small smattering of noise. It continued until they reached the doors. They stepped through, into darkness, and then the sound of it died away. It was quiet. They stood in the dark. Riley's eyes were dry. They stood and they rested. Cal lowered his head. He closed his eyes and leaned into Riley. Riley held him up.

He felt the kid breathing. He felt each breath like it was his own. He stood and he held him tight. There was only this. There was nothing more. He stared into the darkness. He thought in the end this was all that mattered. Nothing more had ever been promised. The kid was heavy against his shoulder. He let him rest. Gently, he pressed his hand to his head. For the last time. He let him rest, and everything was still.

Acknowledgments

Thank you to Judy Heiblum, Wylie O'Sullivan, Clare Conville and Francesca Main; Katherine Zoepf, Sean O'Hagan, Rob Dinsdale, Paul Craig, Jennifer Johns; Sophie Fiennes and Harland Miller.

About the Author

Katie Kitamura was born in 1979, and divides her time between New York and London. *The Longshot* is her first novel.

Reading Group Guide for
THE LONGSHOT

DISCUSSION QUESTIONS

1. A number of times over the course of the story, a certain question comes up: What went wrong in that fateful fight between Cal and Rivera four years ago? Discuss Cal and Riley's conflicting opinions on what actually happened. Who do you think is right?

2. Riley comments that in the beginning of Cal's career, Cal got so used to winning that he just thought it was "the way it was" (p. 16). How did that make losing to Rivera that much harder for him? Why has it taken him so long to get back into serious fighting?

3. What was the result of Murray and Rivera's fight? Do you think Cal would rather follow in Murray's footsteps than risk another defeat by Rivera? Why do you think he chooses to fight him again?

4. Cal and Riley each experience a fight-or-flight impulse during the twenty-four hours leading up to the fight. Why does each of them decide to stay? How do you think the novel would have turned out if one of them had fled? What would it have meant to the one who got left behind?

5. Discuss the dwindling of Riley's optimism over the course of the book. What makes him realize that Cal

should not go into the fight? Why does Riley shut his eyes and say, "Things would have to play out. There was no other way" (p. 150)? In your opinion, was there, in fact, another way?

6. What is Riley's game plan for Cal's fight with Rivera? Why do trainers create a game plan, and why does he think it will work? Does the strategy actually come into play during the real fight?

7. Discuss this statement: "The kid had everything a fighter needed and if he didn't become champion then Riley would have no one to blame but himself" (p. 15). Why does Riley put so much pressure on himself to turn Cal into a champion? Do you think this blindly leads him into believing that Cal can win the rematch?

8. Even though he has never been knocked out, why do you think Cal "guessed he knew the feeling" (p. 23)? Why is it so important to Cal to remain standing in the final fight?

9. Having read Kitamura's work, do you agree with her statement that "there was nothing simple about a fight" (p. 27)? Did *The Longshot* change your perspective on the world of mixed martial arts fighting, on the people involved in it, and on the fighting itself? Why or why not?

10. Do you agree with Kitamura's assertion that "a fight was just a series of logical conclusions" (p.111)? If so, how do you feel about Cal's claim that habit overrides fear, logic and need (p. 139)?

11. Do you think Cal dies at the end of the book? Why or why not?

12. *The Longshot* could have been a much longer story. Why do you think Kitamura chose to keep it short in length and free of much description? How does this choice affect the story's impact? Does it make it more or less powerful? How so?

Author Q&A

1. **How did you become interested in mixed martial arts fighting?**
I was introduced to fighting by my older brother, a tattoo artist who is friendly with (and has done tattoos on) a number of fighters. The first fight I saw—the rematch, for those who follow the sport, between Mirko Filipovic and Kevin Randleman—set something off. In that fight, a powerful narrative was communicated in incredibly economical terms (forty-one seconds, for the record). And I was captivated by the physicality of the fighters, the stories that were evoked in their bodies and movements.

I think I pretty much knew immediately that I wanted to write something about fighting, and my brother was a great guide to the sport. We've been to fights around the world together, watched and rewatched our favorite fights, endlessly debated the strengths and weaknesses of individual fighters. We're pretty extravagantly different; while I was studying for a Ph.D. in American literature he was busy establishing himself as one of the top tattoo artists in the world. But fighting is something we're both completely passionate about. He's now had the word *LONGSHOT* tattooed on his knuckles, and that's the cover image for the book. So the whole thing has come full circle in a really wonderful way.

2. **Where did the inspiration for Cal and Riley come from? Are they based on anyone that you know?**
The individual fighting styles and physical descriptions of Cal, Rivera and Luis are based on fighters that I met while researching the book. It was very useful to have a visual image of the characters while I was writing—in an odd way it helped clarify for me what the characters would or wouldn't do.

I didn't have a specific model for Riley, but in a lot of ways his character emerged as a foil and partner to Cal, so once I had a sense of Cal, it was quite easy to write Riley's character.

3. **Much of the intensity and tempo of *The Longshot* stems from the fact that it takes place over the course of only a few days. Did you ever consider telling a longer, more drawn-out story? Why did you choose to write it the way you did?**
I always wanted to make the book as taut as possible, both in terms of style and structure; I wanted it to come as close as possible to the rhythm and feel of an actual fight. The device of focusing on a fixed period of time was fairly integral to the way I thought about the book from the very beginning.

Having said that, I did at one point consider a radically different structure, whereby the book would be split into two parts. The first half would be told from Cal and Riley's perspective, the second from Rivera's. I went so far as to write out an entirely different second half for the book, but in the end it didn't work.

The experience of watching a fight live is extraordinary. I have to confess that I experience it as an extreme form of anxiety. I end up having a completely irrational, emotional stake in the outcome of a fight—in that sense, I'm a shameless fan.

In total contrast, I'm amazed by how relaxed the fighters themselves are before a fight. Outside the ring they are a disparate group, but on the whole I found them to be smart, funny and extremely generous. They were very open about their experiences, which was useful in researching the book.

8. **Are there certain MMA fighters that you admire? If so, can you tell us a little bit about them?**
I pretty much admire anybody who has the discipline and the will to make a career out of fighting. It takes buckets of nerve. What struck me most was the incredibly public nature of what they were doing. The first fight I saw live, the fighter I was shadowing lost in front of a crowd of forty thousand people. The scale of that is staggering to me. Undergoing that overlap between something very personal and something very public strikes me as both admirable and also somewhat terrifying.

9. **Despite the dangers involved, have you ever thought of stepping into the ring yourself? Or are you more comfortable on the sidelines?**
No, absolutely not. I'm not one to probe my limitations.

10. **What is next for you?**
I'm working on my next book, and researching fish farms.

4. Did you intentionally leave it ambiguous as to whether Cal dies at the end? To *your* mind, did he die? For me, concretely speaking, he doesn't die—but it has been a question for quite a few people, and I'm happy for it to be ambiguous.

5. The events at the end of *The Longshot* are seriously disappointing, if not outright devastating. Did you ever have an alternate ending in mind, wherein Cal won? Or did you know from the start that Rivera was going to win?
It was initially an open question, but the further I got into the writing of the book, the more it seemed apparent that Cal couldn't win, although there were plenty of moments when I wished he could!

6. You have a particular perspective on the athlete/ trainer relationship—you go so far as to write, "A trainer was supposed to protect his fighter. . . . That was the promise. That was what kept a fighter and a trainer together" (p. 144). Have you ever had a close relationship with a trainer, coach, or teacher?
I trained pretty seriously in classical ballet when I was younger, and I think that ended up informing a lot of the book. The idea of physical strain and discipline, the question of how and when you leave that life behind— they're things I'm familiar with on one level or another. And, of course, the relationship with a trainer. It's a relationship that is built on expectation, which is necessary but also rather dangerous.

7. In your capacity as a journalist, you have spent time in the world of MMA, traveling to California and Japan to watch fights and interview fighters. What is it like to watch a fight live? What are the fighters like outside of the ring?